THE OTHER SIDE OF SORROW

Why, in the opinion of her teenage son and daughter, did their mother, Margaret, seem moody and quite out of character during the same few days each year? Why did she secretly engage a private detective to look for a young girl, while her executive husband, Hugh, was away on business in America? Would the attraction of the earthy but sincere Sam Perrett break up her marriage?

JUDY CHARD

THE OTHER SIDE OF SORROW

Complete and Unabridged

LINFORD
Leicester

First published in Great Britain in 1977

First Linford Edition
published 2004

British Library CIP Data

Chard, Judy
    The other side of sorrow.—Large print ed.—
Linford romance library
    1. Love stories
    2. Large type books
    I. Title
    823.9'14 [F]

    ISBN 1–84395–120–7

Published by
F. A. Thorpe (Publishing)
Anstey, Leicestershire

Set by Words & Graphics Ltd.
Anstey, Leicestershire
Printed and bound in Great Britain by
T. J. International Ltd., Padstow, Cornwall

This book is printed on acid-free paper

1

Margaret heard the telephone ring in the hall as she folded the last of Hugh's shirts, spreading it neatly on top of his case.

She stretched out her hand to pick up the bedroom extension, but someone downstairs had beaten her to it.

She waited, holding her breath, expecting a voice to call her, for someone to tell her that a man by the name of John Beckett wanted to speak to her . . . but all she could hear was her daughter Linda's voice — now as she listened to it she thought it was a rather toneless, monotonous sound, the voice had no trace of her own slight cockney intonation. She smiled wrily, obviously they had taken great care to eliminate that at the expensive boarding school she'd attended.

A feeling of relief ran along her

nerves as she realised the call was not hers. She had told the man not to ring until the afternoon, until Hugh had left safely for the airport, but he might have forgotten, particularly if he had some good news for her.

He had seemed rather an ebullient young man, she had even had slight qualms whether it was wise to trust him with such a delicate matter. But she supposed private detectives did have a code of honour and secrecy much as the ordinary police, and he had told her he'd been in the plain clothes branch . . .

She went on with the packing.

It seemed strange in a way to be doing such a chore for Hugh and not for herself as well. In the twenty years they'd been married he'd only been away for the odd night — but now he was going to be in America for at least a couple of months. It was to be an extensive tour of all the states. He had suggested she accompany him, but she had put forward her fear of flying as an excuse, although it hadn't been the basic reason — at last the chance she had been half longing for, half dreading, presented itself — she could make no excuse to herself for not grasping the opportunity with both hands . . . and now the die was cast, all she wanted was for events to start moving . . .

Hugh came from the bathroom which adjoined their room, and she turned as he handed her his silver backed brushes and electric razor.

'Wonder if they have the same plugs in American hotels — for my shaver I mean.'

Margaret rolled up the last pair of socks and tucked them neatly into a corner of the case. 'Isn't it odd that one never thinks about those kind of details normally? But they must of course — how on earth would all the famous jet setters manage not to have a five o'clock shadow, or whatever it's called?'

He grinned at her and drew her hand through his arm, looking down at her with unaccustomed tenderness.

'Will you be all right while I'm away Margaret?'

'Of course, darling.' She gave him a brief hug and then turned away, drawing her arm back, her eyes lowered as a feeling of guilt flooded through her at the touch and his obvious concern. It was almost as if she intended to be unfaithful to him — but actually nothing could have been further from her mind . . .

Two small lines formed between his brows as he said, 'I hope to heaven this demo goes O.K. and that we can establish some good contacts 'State-side', as the mid-Atlantic Whizz kids call it. An awful lot depends on it — maybe the whole future of the firm — specially now we're in the Common Market . . . in a way we have to sell ourselves all over again as part of the European Community. It isn't a popular move with some of the Americans, I think they'd rather have us as one of the States than as we are now,' he shrugged,

4

'still it's an accomplished fact whatever one may think about it . . . '

She wasn't listening. Her mind had swung away into the dream which seemed more and more to claim her every waking moment now.

Suddenly she was impatient for him to be gone, to be left free . . .

As if he sensed her slight impatience, he snapped the locks on the case and took a last look round.

She followed him from the room and down the shallow staircase, across the hall where everything spoke discreetly, but obviously of a comfortable income and good taste — the polished floor, the expensive rugs, the lavish arrangements of hot house flowers and potted plants. The front door stood open with a backdrop of neatly manicured lawns and rose beds, the sweep of sanded drive, and the hot summer smell of new mown grass and myriad perfume of flowers . . . a drowsy bee droned, bumbling, among the deep red roses in the silver bowl on the chest in the hall — giving a feeling of normality, of continuity to the scene ... a scene which she was about to change, to lift from the normal — perhaps for ever, who could tell ...

He bent and kissed her gently on the lips, preoccupied now with the immediate future into which all his thoughts were projected — the call of business, his all absorbing life which left him no time for a hobby, for recreation or his family — beyond their well being and needs, he prided himself on being a good provider ...

With a banging of doors, the shining, chauffeur-driven car slid away, down the drive, out through the wrought iron gates, up the side road and was immediately absorbed into the hum of traffic which raced ceaselessly by on the nearby motorway ...

Margaret stood for a moment, her fingers on her lips where he had kissed her — thinking how once his touch had brought little jets of excitement, and then a mounting passion — but never a fulfilment like once she had known . . . before . . .

She turned and looked up at the house — pseudo Tudor someone had once said, built on the costly fringe of the city — the dry martini belt — within easy reach of the shops, and yet sufficiently secluded to give the owners the impression at least of country peace and quiet — apart from the jets which screamed overhead with ever increasing regularity . . .

This was her home — and sometimes she marvelled how far she had come from the sleazy back streets of her childhood — here she lived with a husband who was not exactly a tycoon, but a brilliant business man — but a husband who had gradually slipped away from her, preoccupied as a person — or was it the other way round? Her home, and that of a couple of teenage kids to whom it was little more than an hotel which cost them nothing and was convenient . . .

Was this really what life was all

about? This cushioned existence from the outside world that money brought . . .

She heard the phone ring again, and hurried through the door. As she crossed the hall her daughter Linda came down the stairs two at a time and seized the receiver before she could reach it.

Tall and fair, not yet showing the plumpness of her mother, but with the same clear skin and fine hair. But already, at sixteen, she was a stranger to her parents. Once she had been Hugh's Golden Girl, running to him with all her problems — then almost over night it seemed, she had become changed — secretive, arrogant, defiant . . .

She held out the phone to her mother.

'It's for you — some dishy-sounding bloke who won't give his name . . . surprise surprise . . . and Pop not even on the aeroplane yet . . . '

Then no longer interested as the call was not for her, she went back up the stairs humming a pop tune.

Margaret's heart did a somersault, although she had been expecting, longing for the call, now it had materialised she hovered on the threshold of the future, of the unknown . . .

'Mrs Gennert here — who is this please?'

'John Beckett,' the voice replied. She felt the hot colour flood her face as though unseen ears were listening and she arranging a clandestine meeting with her lover . . .

'Oh yes Mr Beckett. I hope you have some news for me, good news . . . '

'I've traced your daughter . . . '

The words seemed to sizzle along the line and then hang in letters of fire for all the world to see . . . she couldn't reply, could hardly think coherently. It was as if the ground had been swept from under her feet . . .

'Hullo — are you still there?' There was an undertone of impatience now . . .

'Yes, yes I'm here — it's just that you

seem to have been very quick, it's a little bit of a shock . . . but thank you. Perhaps you'd give me the details.'

She pulled the note pad and pencil towards her and wrote down as he spoke.

'She's working at the Pack Horse Hotel, Queensbridge in Devon. Actually I'm staying there myself but I didn't know exactly what you'd want to do. I can book you a room if you like — for a couple of nights or whatever you wish,' he paused, then added in a low voice, 'it's a pretty rough and ready kind of place, not up your street I should imagine. But there is a better place at the top of the main street if you'd rather . . . '

'No, no,' she broke in quickly, 'please book me in and I'll get the first train I can.' She hadn't finished speaking before she started to turn the leaves of the railway time-table that stood by the phone as though through swift action she could project herself immediately into the train . . .

'I imagine you don't want to use your own name . . . '

'I . . . ' she hesitated, 'no, perhaps it would be better. Choose anything you like.' She had to smile, it all somehow smacked of the cloak and dagger books . . .

'There's another thing — if you're not coming by road you won't be able to get a train straight through, you'll have to go to Plymouth and I'll meet you there. Perhaps you'd ring me back when you know the time of the train . . . '

She looked up trains, rang him back, made all the necessary arrangements in a kind of dreamlike state. She had burned her boats, there was no going back, the impulse that drove her would never be satisfied until she had seen her daughter, spoken to her . . . she wasn't quite sure why she had decided to go by train — it had been instinctive — the journey must be as anonymous as possible — a car could so easily be traced . . .

She went slowly up the stairs . . . Linda was lying on her bed with the door ajar but her small transistor was blaring out pop music so she couldn't have possibly heard her conversation. She flicked through the pages of a glossy magazine, rolling over to face her mother as she heard her step on the landing.

'I'm going to Scotland for a few days, Mum. Shan't be back this side of the week-end.'

Margaret looked at her with unseeing eyes.

The girl didn't notice, she yawned, stretched and said, 'I take it Dad's gone . . .'

Her mother nodded. She was tempted to say, 'I think you could have been around to say goodbye.' But thought better of it. What was the use. Neither of the children could have cared less it seemed — what their parents did, whether they saw them or not.

Tim — two years older than Linda,

had hitched to Geneva yesterday to visit some racing driver pal who lived there. He spent all his time chasing his idols in motor racing — Europe, America, Japan — wherever took his fancy. It was an obsession, taking all his time and energy, for he knew the details of every driver, every Formula of every car and the history of their individual performances.

'Anyone would think I was a millionaire the way that boy burns up cash,' Hugh would sigh as the bills rolled in.

Margaret went on to her own room. Linda glanced after her for a moment, some surprise on her face. She'd expected some comment on the fact she hadn't been there to see her father off. She'd forgotten as a matter of fact, she'd been over at the local stables looking at a new hunter she was thinking of buying . . .

After a moment she shrugged her shoulders and turned back to the magazine, glancing first at the date on her automatic watch . . . of course, the 22nd July — the day Mum always went a bit odd, moody and vague. Tim always called it 'The old girl's broody time,' and Muriel Grailey, the house-keeper, fussed round, keeping the family at bay at these times. She seemed to be the only one Margaret would tolerate for the few days either side of that particular day . . .

Now Margaret went to the big cupboard that ran along the whole length of one wall of her bedroom, and got out her small case and the big hand-bag she used for carrying odds and ends of make-up, a change of undies and so on if she went away for the night.

She was so absorbed in selecting the things she felt necessary that she didn't hear footsteps on the thickly carpeted passage as the grey-haired woman came to stand in the doorway.

She opened her note case. There was about a hundred pounds in notes and change, and her cheque book, credit cards . . .

There had been an awkward moment when Hugh had been going through the bank statements just before he left, and wanted to know what on earth she had drawn over two hundred pounds in cash for, usually she bought her clothes on charge accounts, and he paid all the household bills.

'I might go away for a few days, visit some of my friends . . . '

It had of course been to pay John Beckett his expenses and fee in advance . . .

'Going away are you?'

She jumped and swung round guiltily. 'I didn't hear you. Come in and close the door, Linda's in her room.'

For a moment she sat looking at Muriel Grailey's reflection in the triple mirror on her dressing table. She still had a slim figure and young face — in fact she looked little different from the sixteen odd years when they had first met. She'd been with Margaret ever since Linda had been born. The baby had nearly cost her her life, and when she left the hospital the doctor had suggested she should have some home help . . .

Her mind scurried back down the years. She and Hugh had been thrilled at the birth of a girl to make the pigeon pair with Tim, as he had put it. In those days all she had wanted was his love and approval, her home and the children . . . it was only later this great longing, this hunger had consumed her, to find that other child had become like an addiction eating into her life. Was it because she didn't have enough to occupy her time — or because their love had become a matter of routine . . .

She could remember the excitement she had felt when he walked up between the beds of the long maternity ward, looking handsome, fresh, and even then somehow glowing with the success that was to come.

Some of the other mothers had

followed his progress towards her with envious eyes — and she'd been reminded of that very first time she'd lain in a maternity ward when things had been so different — then she'd been ashamed, guilty — whereas now she too glowed with pride.

Muriel was one of the ward cleaners and they'd struck up a friendship. They used to chat as she tidied Margaret's locker, and something had clicked between them so that when the doctor had told Hugh she'd need some help with the other small child, and the new baby she had asked if she could have Muriel, and he had leapt at the idea, for one thing it solved the problem of the slight feeling of neglect for Margaret he had when he brought home work in the evenings, and the late hours he often spent at the office.

Muriel was a widow with no ties and she had taken to the rather lonely girl who at the time seemed a little out of her depth, for Hugh was already on the bottom rungs of the ladder to success in the small engineering business where he'd started as an apprentice. Work fascinated, absorbed him, and the desire to make money and succeed, drove him remorselessly.

A warm friendship had developed between the women and probably Muriel Grailey knew Margaret better than anyone — but even she had never been told about that first baby. Apart from Margaret's mother, no one had known, and that half of the secret had died with her, for she had made her daughter swear never to tell Hugh.

But it hadn't escaped Muriel's notice that each year the 22nd July brought some kind of tension to Margaret, she became withdrawn and moody, unlike herself, and automatically she had protected her from the others, guessing it was the anniversary of something painful — and she'd had a shrewd idea what that something could be . . .

Now Margaret started to brush her hair . . . 'I'm going away for a few days because a private detective has found

18

my daughter,' she said slowly . . . 'my elder daughter,' she added . . .

Muriel nodded.

'I thought you might have guessed,' Margaret continued, 'so now I might as well tell you the facts. I know I don't have to ask you to keep them to yourself.' She paused for a moment, as if remembering was painful.

'My parents kept a back street pub in the East End of London — till my father was killed in some kind of brawl, then mother took in lodgers. Mike was one of them. A commercial traveller. At eighteen I fell in love with him, madly, wildly, totally . . . whatever he did was right by me . . . '

Saying his name brought back the memory of those blue eyes, blue as zircons — she'd read that description in one of the women's magazines which she read by torchlight under the bedclothes, for her mother would have been disgusted with what she called 'that cheap trash'.

She was incurably romantic and

entirely unsophisticated because of her strict upbringing, and the combination of Irish blarney, with an expertise in the art of making love, had swept her off her feet when Mike appeared.

The lilacs had been in bloom the evening they met — heady with perfume even in the sooty, dirty, main street. Someone had a window box of wallflowers, and the summer heat of the spring evening had shimmered on the hot city pavements. She'd been on her way home from the greengrocery shop where she worked, and he had drawn up his car at the kerb, winding down the window and leaning out, grinning — his teeth had reminded her of the peeled almonds they sold in the shop . . .

She'd seen him briefly in the dining room at the back of the pub when he arrived, but this was the first time they'd spoken. 'If you're as hot and thirsty as I am, Meg, how about a drink? Just a tiny one,' he held up thumb and forefinger, measuring. She'd had to laugh at the sheer cheek of him. And no one else had ever called her Meg before ... neither had she ever drunk whisky before — only a glass of cooking sherry at Christmas. He told her it was mostly ginger ale and ice.

After the second one she didn't care. Vaguely she remembered driving out into the dusk laden countryside, there were lambs in the fields, the grass was greener than she believed possible.

He stopped where the trees formed a green arch, almost like a church, overhead. He'd spread a tartan rug beneath them, so that as they lay on the soft ground she could see the dark blue of the sky above his head, and the beginning of a moon — a silver sickle ...

The first time they made love had been frightening, suffocating, painful and yet in a way too, full of wonder. But as the weeks stretched into summer and he taught her the ways of love, she responded to his desire, only waiting for the day when he would ask her to marry him.

If her mother guessed what was going on, she said nothing. Looking after the lodgers, keeping an eye on the barman who was sticky fingered, and trying to make ends meet drained her of all emotion, all energy — and in spite of her husband's temper, she'd loved him and his death had left her bereft. Anyway she had brought Margaret up so strictly she was certain the girl had no idea of original sin or what the word sex meant . . .

It was just before Christmas that Margaret realised things were not as they should be when she looked at the calendar . . . she told Mike, wondering if she might be pregnant. He'd laughed and told her it just wasn't possible . . . and she had believed him, and gone all innocent to the family doctor, who had told her bluntly she was two months pregnant and she'd better get the father to marry her quick before it showed . . .

All she could think of was the words

to choose to tell her mother . . . dragging her feet through the foggy December streets . . . first she'd tell Mike, probably it would only be a matter of days, weeks at the most, before arrangements could be made for the wedding, it would have to be a quiet one, still that didn't really matter . . .

It didn't seem possible he could just disappear like a puff of smoke. It was as though he'd never existed, as if he'd been a figment of her imagination. His firm had no forwarding address, he'd asked for his cards and left . . .

For a moment as she formed the words, she thought her mother would strike her. Her face suffused with a scarlet anger, then she seemed to crumple up as she collapsed into a chair, throwing her apron over her head, sobbing, shouting, screaming obscenities at Margaret.

'You filthy little tart, bringing your nasty dirty ways to this house . . . as if I haven't enough to put up with — and you no help . . .'

Margaret had cringed like a beaten puppy in front of this unrecognisable woman, for she had never seen her mother in such a rage before . . . and then the ultimate disgrace, she'd been sick on the parlour floor . . .

For days the row had raged up and down stairs, out of the hearing of the bar and the other lodgers, until at last, weary and drained, Margaret had been driven even to thoughts of suicide . . . then realising what she had done, how far she had pushed the girl, her mother said, 'I've written to your Aunt Doris in Birmingham, she'll let you stay there till the child's born, then you can come back here — at least then the neighbours won't know . . . '

And so the baby had been taken to an orphanage without Margaret even seeing it, all she knew was it had been a girl . . . and she had come back to the sleazy back street . . .

Now Muriel stood looking down at her, her eyes filled with compassion. 'So you don't know if the baby was adopted . . . you poor child.' She put her arms round Margaret, 'no wonder this time has been difficult for you to bear,' she paused, 'but what I can't quite see is why this sudden decision, after all these years, to find the girl. Is it wise?'

'Today she is twenty one,' Margaret said slowly, her voice hardly above a whisper, 'a milestone in anyone's life. And now I've the money and the opportunity, with Hugh away — I must see her Muriel. All these years I've longed to know what she looks like, what she's doing, what kind of girl she is. Everything about her.

'Each year I've thought more and more about her, so when Hugh said he had to go abroad it seemed as if Fate had arranged it.'

Muriel nodded slowly, 'I understand — and this detective, is he discreet?'

'Yes I think so, he was invalided out of the CID with just a small pension.'

'But what possible help could you give him, what facts to go on?'

'That's just it. Very little. Really only the name of the orphanage and the date of the baby's birth . . . but he's managed it, it seems almost too good to be true.'

'And shall you tell her that you are her mother?'

Margaret swung round. 'No never, she must never know, it wouldn't be fair,' she hesitated a moment, 'not fair on either of us . . . '

'I see,' the other woman said slowly, 'and is it that you are hoping to find something in her that you feel you are missing out on?'

Margaret looked down at her clenched hands. 'Perhaps, although my two kids are normal enough I suppose, I know these days it's the fashion to use the home as a bed and breakfast place, I know they don't really need me, any more than Hugh does.' Her eyes slid away from Muriel's gaze.

'Someone said the other day that out of ten married women, four are unhappy, three are just existing and

26

only three are happy. I think he was right. It's a fact we must accept. Maybe it is because of all the time I spend on my own that I have dwelt increasingly on the idea of my other child . . . the one who may need me.'

Muriel's eyes were bright with tears as she said, 'Leave me your telephone number. If the children want to know I'll tell them you're visiting friends. But I'd better know where you are just in case of emergency.'

She bent and kissed Margaret on the cheek.

'And good luck with your quest. I only hope this unknown girl turns out to be all you ask of her . . . '

She turned and went swiftly from the room.

2

Margaret was not impressed with the outward appearance of the Pack Horse Inn . . .

It stood halfway down the steep hill that was the main shopping street of Queensbridge — a small Devon market town.

She had had a hot and tiring journey, and then the traffic on the road from Plymouth had been a constant stream, many of the cars towing boats and caravans, making John Beckett concentrate on his driving, which in itself left much to be desired, so that her feet had nearly been through the floor-boards on several occasions.

They spoke very little on the way — partly possibly through an unspoken but mutual desire to get to the hotel before any details were discussed, so that it was with some relief when they drew up in front of the Inn.

At first glance it held a certain enchantment, for it was obviously very old, and probably originally a coaching inn for an archway above a cobbled alleyway led to a yard at the back, but the outside badly needed a coat of paint, to add to the air of desolation and neglect, a few miserable shrubs and plants wilted sadly in tubs on the pavement by the door, and as they pushed open the entrance door the smell of stale cooking permeated the tiny foyer.

Margaret felt the depression which had been threatening ever since she'd arrived at Plymouth, descending like a heavy cloud, bringing a throbbing pain behind her eyes . . .

There was a small reception counter, behind which stood a woman whom she judged to be a little younger than herself. Her hair was tinted a rather harsh shade of red, her plump figure reluctantly squeezed into a black satin dress with the inevitable string of imitation pearls. Her make-up looked as though she had laid it on with a trowel and was now suffering from the summer heat . . .

She raised pencilled brows at Margaret, who had come in alone while John drove the car into the yard at the back.

'Can I help you, Madam?'

'I have a room booked, Mr Beckett arranged it,' Margaret replied.

At this piece of information the woman's brows all but disappeared under the curled fringe as she shot a curious glance at Margaret.

I suppose she thinks I'm his fancy piece, Margaret said to herself with a flash of amusement, still, she shouldn't show it in quite such an obvious manner even if she does. I would have thought at her age and in this kind of job she'd have got used to dealing with some rather queer situations . . .

The woman ran her finger down the register and Margaret noticed the bright-red nail polish was chipped, revealing a none too clean fingernail . . .

'Mrs Smith?' The tone now had become patronising and disbelieving . . .

Margaret nodded. She had to admit it was a bit obvious, she would have thought a man who was a detective could have had a little more imagination in choosing a name. Under different circumstances she would have remarked so to John Beckett when he had imparted the information to her in the car . . . but now she felt too preoccupied to bother . . .

An old man in a stained white steward's jacket and baggy black trousers showed her to her room.

As he opened the door the stale air felt as oppressive as an oven, the net curtains at the windows had shrunk and yellowed from many washings. On investigation the bed was lumpy and the springs creaked . . . she went over to the window and looked out.

The view was breathtaking. Across the uneven roofs of the old town buildings she could see the distant fields of the rolling Devon countryside, some still lush and green with cattle grazing, some shaved to a pale tea colour where the hay had been cut and carried, and some, where the breeze ruffled the corn like golden watered silk . . . she imagined she could smell the warm summer perfume of it all . . . her heart lifted a little. Maybe she would have time to explore some of the high banked lanes she remembered from childhood holidays . . .

But at the moment she had other things on her mind.

She thanked the old man and pressed a fifty penny piece into his hand. With a naivete she found rather attractive, he gazed at it lying in his palm, one would have thought he'd never seen such a thing before, she could imagine that usually the patrons of the Pack Horse didn't go in much for tipping . . .

'Thank 'ee Missis,' he said, backing through the door and closing it softly behind him. Margaret wouldn't have been at all surprised if he'd touched an imaginary forelock . . .

Now she unpacked the few clothes she had brought, and washed in the soft, peaty water which ran lukewarm from the hot tap. Then she went down to dinner.

John had reserved a table near the window overlooking the main street, and directly they had given their order he wasted no time in telling her what she was longing to hear . . .

'She's called Teresa — apparently any children taken into the Orphanage — which was run by nuns incidentally — were given a saint's name. They tagged Brown on the end, goodness knows where they got that from . . . '

Margaret gave a half-hearted smile. 'Poor child — it isn't much better than the one you chose for me,' she said. For a moment he looked a little taken aback, then he gave her a bleak answering smile. She felt that he, like Queen Victoria, was not amused . . . 'Teresa Brown,' she said softly, 'I wonder if anyone ever calls her Tess or Terry . . . '

'I should rather doubt it — she looks . . . ' he hesitated as if he'd just remembered he was talking about his client's daughter and chose his words more carefully, 'er, a little bit severe perhaps, unapproachable — this maybe because she has had to look after herself . . . '

Little did he realise his words were like a small dagger in Margaret's heart . . . it was her doing that the girl had been alone . . . she knew that only too well.

Now she looked round. 'If she works here, what does she do? Have I seen her yet, you haven't told me what her position in the hotel is. Obviously she's not the receptionist cum manageress — I've already met her . . . '

'She's a chambermaid,' John said quietly, 'in fact,' he went on, 'you could say *the* chambermaid, they only have one. She comes on duty about 6.30 in the morning, works till lunch time, has the afternoon off, and then comes on again in the evening.'

'Sounds like slave labour to me,' she said shortly, thinking the proprietor was obviously out to get the maximum from his meagre staff . . . A chambermaid . . . now she had come all this way, waited for so long, Margaret was suddenly desperate for a sight of her daughter, as though all the longing down the years had telescoped into this one moment in time . . .

Teresa . . . she repeated the name over and over again to herself. She couldn't quite decide whether she liked it or not — it was the kind of name one didn't feel strongly about either way . . . she wouldn't have chosen it herself . . . suddenly she realised she had no right to question the choice . . .

John was telling her the details of his enquiries . . . she tried to listen, but her mind kept wandering away, as did her eyes to the open door into the hall as she wondered if the girl would come through the foyer to go on duty . . . it was hardly likely, she'd use the back entrance through the yard . . .

'I started of course at the Orphanage, at the address you gave me in Dudhampton,' John said. 'It had been pulled down to build some ring road or other round the town, but fortunately the local vicar knew where the new building was.' He paused, 'Vicars are among my best informants on practically any subject where tracing people is concerned . . . anyway she'd left the Orphanage of the Sacred Heart when she was seventeen — according to their records, although I must say they weren't too anxious to tell me . . . it seems she hadn't shown any particular flair for anything special . . . '

'You mean they said she wasn't very bright,' Margaret said shortly. She sipped the wine she'd ordered. It should have been cooled, but the same man who had been the porter, was now the waiter and obviously knew nothing about such niceties. But she didn't want to make a fuss, draw unnecessary attention to herself and John. As she drank it she thought resignedly that a few years ago she wouldn't have known any better herself . . . it was among the many things Hugh had taught her . . .

'Well of course I can't say anything about that side of her — but it does seem she drifted rather from one job to another. The Orphanage started her off as a nursemaid, but she didn't stick that for long — impatient with the children they said . . . '

Maybe she was envious of the warm home life they had, which she had been denied . . . Margaret thought rue-fully . . .

'Then she served in a shop, behind a bar, in a transport café — what actually brought her eventually to Devon I don't know, probably the summer season and an advert in a Midland paper, I believe the west country hoteliers do often advertise in that area for seasonal staff . . . '

'I shouldn't have thought they'd get many summer visitors here,' Margaret said, glancing round at the threadbare carpet, the stained table cloths, and the waiter who was busily scratching his ear with a pencil as he tried to add up a bill . . .

'Possibly not, but school holidays start in July as you know, and this is a good centre for the moors and the sea. I suppose even this kind of place has its clientele. Anyway I had quite a job to persuade them to let me have a room for you.'

'Who owns the place, is it a brewery house?' she asked as the waiter brought the coffee they had ordered. It might equally well have been tea . . .

'A fellow called Sam Perrett, although he doesn't seem to be around much. I've only seen him a couple of times. I found him rather brash, looks more like a bookie than a hotelier, and you could cut his Yorkshire accent with a very blunt knife. Usually west country folk are a bit allergic to the north — unless they happen to be on holiday. I wouldn't think he's used to this kind of trade either — I would think he'd be more at home in a town pub and in the back streets at that . . . ' He looked down at his coffee as he stirred in two spoonfuls of sugar. Just as well for he didn't catch the expression on Margaret's face as she thought what he would say if she told him his rich client had started in life in exactly such a pub as he visualised for Sam Perrett . . . But she simply said, 'I can see the police training coming out in you Mr Beckett.'

He grinned, 'It's odd really you know, I got fed up with routine in the Force, was glad to leave in a way, but now I have even more to cope with, people think being a private detective is all glamour, but most of it's hard slogging and paper work.' He broke off. 'Here comes Sam now, want me to introduce you?'

Margaret had no time to answer as the stocky, rather florid man made his way over to their table.

'Good evening Mrs Smith, Mr Beckett. I hope everything is to your satisfaction. On holiday are you? Or come for the races?' He grinned broadly, his face bronzed and alive. Margaret's immediate reaction was that here was a man who looked at least as if he lived every moment of every day . . . he's got nice teeth . . . she thought, inconsequently. And nice eyes. He's a bit flashy — not much 'couth' as Linda would say. But nor did I have once . . . maybe that's the mistake I've made with the kids, giving them too much 'couth', making them better than I am . . .

She smiled back. This was Teresa's employer. She needed to gain his confidence, his approval . . . Sam was rubbing his hands together now. He wore a diamond ring on the little finger of his right hand. Margaret wondered briefly if he was married, where his wife was . . . 'Lovely weather, though too hot for some . . . '

She realised he was trying to make conversation while his eyes took in her expensive suit, the crocodile hand-bag, the wedding ring . . .

'We get a lot of folk stay here for the races at Bushel — like it better than the town as you might say, good for business, are races . . . '

His Yorkshire accent grew thicker with his enthusiasm, and a certain rather endearing anxiety to please . . .

Margaret was certain he referred to money as 'brass', and called the female staff 'lass'. He reminded her of a stocky brindled bull terrier she'd once had. He too had looked a bit rough and ready, but underneath was soft as candy floss. She wondered if he was the same. Now, realising that Margaret and her companion wished to be alone he said good evening and regretted he must leave them as he had important papers to attend to . . .

They decided to wander outside for a breath of fresh air. And Margaret had a faint hope, both ridiculous and unreasonable she knew, that they might bump into Teresa in the street. Queensbridge couldn't have contained

more than a few thousand inhabitants
. . . it seemed a lifetime to have to wait
till the morning . . . John had discovered by some devious method that this
was her half day so she wouldn't be
coming on duty before the morning
. . . now, womanlike. Margaret longed
to ask John to describe her daughter in
detail, but managed to curb her
curiosity. She knew anyway his replies
would be manlike, unobservant and
unsatisfactory . . .

When they returned to the hotel
the place seemed deserted. Margaret
decided an early night was indicated
— she felt somehow drained, both
mentally and physically . . . she started
up the stairs and as she did so, glanced
through the glass topped door which
led to the manager's office.

She was rather taken aback to see the
manageress clasped tightly in Sam's
arms as they kissed . . . the 'important
papers' he had to deal with, she
thought. Although it was none of her
business, for some inexplicable reason it

surprised her to think the forthright man he had appeared to be, could have succumbed to the rather cheap charms of that woman . . . she shrugged her shoulders. After all she'd only met him briefly but there was something she'd liked about him, something which made her feel he was above that kind of thing with a woman not worthy of him . . .

I'm letting my imagination run away with me she thought — good heavens, it's ridiculous, almost as if I were a jealous schoolgirl . . .

It took her a long time to get to sleep in the unaccustomed hardness of the bed, and even the air which came through the open window was heavy with thunder . . . as she lay staring at the ceiling she realised with a guilty feeling that she hadn't given one thought to Hugh since he'd driven off to the airport, neither had she to Muriel or the children . . . but as she turned on her side she told herself — never mind — I'll think about all that tomorrow . . .

And then, after longing for this day for so many years, after all the elaborate arrangements she'd made, she was asleep when the tap came on the door. It was so light that at first she thought it was part of her dream. Then it was repeated more insistently, and as she struggled up through the haze of sleep trying to remember where she was, she called 'Come in!' and the memories crowded back . . . her eyes focused in the bright light on the figure of the girl standing before her . . . here, grown up, was the baby she had held only within her and never seen, the child she had carried for nine months . . . she wanted to leap out of bed and run over to the girl. Every fibre of her body screamed at her to shout out 'I'm your mother!'

She gripped the blankets till her knuckles showed white. She blinked her eyes so that the gathering tears would go away — so that she could see Teresa properly.

As she looked she realised it would have been almost impossible for anyone to give a vivid description of such a complete plain Jane, her clothes too did little to help, nor did the truculent expression on her face. She wasn't exactly drab even, just nondescript, the kind of girl you'd pass in the street without a backward glance.

Margaret's heart went out to her and just for a moment she couldn't help comparing her with Linda, golden haired with a faintly tanned skin and blue eyes — Linda who had everything money could buy — and this girl who had been deprived even of love all her life . . .

As if she sensed she was being scrutinised — and resented it — the girl now stared back, a kind of defiance in her eyes, the corners of her mouth drooped. Quickly she put down the tray, spilling the milk from the jug as she did so. If she noticed what she'd done, she made no comment, no effort to apologise.

'Thank you, Teresa,' Margaret said, hoping the use of her name by a stranger might provoke at least some response, but if she was surprised she hid her feelings and turned away, her mouth now set in a hard line.

Margaret longed to get her to talk, to hear her voice, but she could think of nothing to say, to ask for . . . Teresa left as anonymously as she had entered. Margaret's tea remained untouched on the table by the bed as she stared through the open window at the sunlight. Her mind and heart were in a turmoil as she tried to recreate a picture of the girl's face, but it eluded her . . . at least she had a nice skin, fine like her own, her eyes were dark, brown she supposed. She couldn't recall exactly what Mike himself had looked like now, down all those years. But she did remember the truculent look, he had had the same expression as his daughter — although then she hadn't used such a harsh word to describe it — the same shadowed eyes . . . tears were near again — she longed to be a mother to this lonely girl at last, to give her all the things she had never had, to restore her confidence, to bring a smile to her lips. But she was determined to stick to her original resolve, never to tell her, certain that if she did she would lose her forever . . .

As she dressed she heard raised voices in the next bedroom.

At first she thought it must be other guests, but then she realised the unmistakable Yorkshire accent was Sam's — and the voice of the manageress . . . they were having an almighty row, and somehow, inexplicably, a little bubble of satisfaction started to rise within her.

It was while they were eating breakfast, and John Beckett had just said that if she had no further need of him, he'd like to get back to London, that some kind of rumpus seemed to be taking place in the hall. Voices were raised, and through the open door they could see a man in a check cap and polo sweater who so obviously spent his life with horses that he could only be either a jockey or a trainer from the nearby racecourse.

He was banging his fist on the counter as he said 'I've stayed in this pub every race meeting for years, it's been a permanent, understood arrangement, long before you people took over. So how can you possibly have let my room to someone else?'

Sam stood to one side, bristling, but trying to keep the peace, while the manageress, her eyes red and puffy and her elaborate hair-do the worse for neglect, was protesting it was none of her fault . . .

'If people don't make proper reservations in the correct manner, then I'm sure it's not my place to think for them. You can't expect Ritz treatment in this sort of place.'

Margaret thought Sam was going to boil over at the slight to his hotel. It was obvious the woman was trying to get her own back for being worsened in what Margaret imagined must have been a lovers' tiff which she had overheard upstairs.

Afterwards she couldn't have possibly said what motivated her — why she did it, she was hardly conscious even of getting up from the table, of leaving the dining room. But she found herself standing by Sam, putting her hand on his arm as if to calm and reassure him.

He swung round, about to shake her off. Then he saw who it was . . .

'Mr Perrett, I'm sorry to intrude, but I couldn't help hearing this gentleman saying he wanted a room, and that there seemed to have been a slight confusion over the booking,' now she looked straight at the manageress who glared back, tossing her head in defiance . . .

'It isn't my fault . . . '

'I don't suppose really it's anyone's fault, not deliberately anyway — just one of those unfortunate things that can happen to any of us. But maybe I can help.

'Mr Beckett has been recalled to London on business, so his room will be empty. I'm sure he won't mind going upstairs now and packing so the room can be got ready for this gentleman.' Margaret turned and smiled at the jockey.

He grinned back. 'Now that's what I call horse sense, if you'll pardon the expression. Why couldn't someone have said that in the first place?'

He relaxed, pushing his cap to the back of his head. 'Just come off the plane and I need a bit of kip before the races — you know how it is, what with keeping the old weight down, and being starving hungry and tired — well perhaps I did blow my top a bit more than necessary . . . '

But now, instead of leaving well alone, the manageress, seeing the opportunity to justify herself said 'There you are, I told you it wasn't my fault . . . '

Sam rounded on her, his face scarlet, obviously at the end of his tether. 'I've had about enough of your cheek and inefficiency my girl, and this puts the lid on it. You can get upstairs and pack your things and all. You're doing this place more harm than good, treating customers like that . . . '

A sly expression came over the woman's face. 'You engaged me by the month, so that'll mean four weeks' wages . . . ' Her tone indicated she was sure Sam's resources wouldn't run to such a sum.

Without another word he strode into the office and came back with a handful of notes, which he thrust at the woman. 'There you are, and you can collect your cards later, now get out . . . '

He turned back to Margaret. 'I can't thank you enough for your help. I only wish I had someone about the place with your tact,' he smiled, 'how about taking on the job, eh?'

How his face changed when he smiled, she thought, like sunshine after rain. It's a nice face, a face you could trust . . .

'Looks though I got to find someone, and quick,' he said slowly.

Suddenly she realised what an opportunity was being offered to her. This could be the excuse to be with Teresa, to make the girl's life a little more bearable, to get to know her even, on a more equal footing than the present one of staff and guest . . .

'I'm in a right pickle, choose how,' Sam was going on, his brow furrowed once more. 'I just don't seem to have the knack somehow, 'tis true, there's nought so queer as folk . . . ' He turned towards the office. Margaret followed him.

'Mr Perrett, just a moment, did you really mean what you said, about offering me a job as manageress?'

He swung round. The expression of disbelief and amazement on his face was so comical that Margaret had difficulty not to burst out laughing. Somehow she guessed his pride would be hurt . . .

'I meant it lass, all right, sure as Christmas is coming I meant it,' he said deliberately.

'Then I'll take you up on it — choose how,' she smiled at him quickly, before either he or she should change their minds . . .

3

As the full impact of what she had just committed herself to, was borne in upon Margaret, she felt numb, dizzy, unreal as if she stood apart watching characters in a play in which she had no role . . .

She had grabbed at Sam's half joking suggestion, thinking only of how a job as manageress would further her relationship with her daughter . . .

Now she started to realise what she had done — acted on impulse — committed herself to a job she knew nothing about, with a man she had only met on the most casual of terms — and a complete reversal of the relationship of employer and employed . . .

She could see that Sam was like a bull in a china shop, he'd got no idea of how to handle either staff or customer, but her own reaction had been instinctive, without careful thought, that she had to acknowledge.

For a moment the thought struck her that it might be more than a desire just to be near Teresa that had prompted her. Had her heart ruled her head? It was hard to say, but whatever the reason, or lack of it, whatever the motive, she had landed the job, she couldn't, wouldn't go back on her word now.

Suddenly she saw the last few years of her life — the time she had been married to Hugh — with a special clarity and insight. In a way she supposed she had lived a lie with him — not that he didn't know about her humble background — although by the time they met she had gravitated from the greengrocer's shop in the East End, to a flower shop within the foyer of one of London's West End Hotels.

She had discovered a natural gift for handling and arranging flowers, and had seen the advertisement for an assistant in the local paper. She had gone to the interview, never expecting to be accepted, to stand a chance among the sophisticated girls she imagined lining up — but the manager had liked her quiet manner and simple politeness, and felt sure most of his rather jaded customers would do likewise — she had a kind of freshness that was spring like.

It was through this job that she had met Hugh. At the time he'd been a struggling young executive, without much money to spare, and he'd wanted some flowers for the Sales Director's wife at the conference he was attending.

Margaret had suggested violets — they were about the cheapest flowers in the shop . . . 'They have a lovely perfume, and most women like flowers that smell nice,' she'd said, smiling at the young man who seemed almost as shy as herself, and quite unlike most of the men who frequented the shop, wanting exotic hot house plants for wife or mistress — usually as a peace offering.

To the surprise of them both, impulsively he had invited her out to dinner — she had accepted — and that had started their association — an odd one for those days for he came from a poor but professional and proud family — as different from Margaret's background as chalk from cheese — but she had grown genuinely to love him and tried to educate herself to his standard and now even she had to admit she'd made a passable job of it . . .

But there had still been times when she longed to relax, to revert to type even — mentally as it were to kick of her high heeled, expensive shoes and push her feet into old, well worn slippers . . . but always there had been a position to keep up, important clients to impress and entertain, and more and more Hugh had had to go abroad. They saw less and less of each other, grew apart as the years passed. Maybe it happened with most married couples she supposed, but there were times when someone like Sam crossed her path for a few brief moments — comfortable, relaxing kind of people with whom she felt perfectly at home, and a nostalgia for what might have been filled her . . . usually to be dismissed as quickly as it had occurred . . .

And now as if he half realised some of the turmoil in her mind, Sam took her arm and led her gently into his office, closing the door behind him.

'Now, lass, sit there and I'll get you a drink, we both need a good stiff one.' He went over to a wall cupboard and took down a bottle and two glasses.

Margaret shook her head. 'Not for me thanks, I'm not much of a drinker at the best of times, but I could do with a cup of tea.' She was tempted to add, 'and if I were you I'd stick to tea as well, you're going to need all your wits about you to deal with that madam of a manageress before she's off the premises,' but she bit back the words. After all it was really no business of hers, and if she was going to remain in the capacity of a member of the staff, she'd better get used to the idea right away.

She sipped the hot, sweet tea Sam had got for her.

'I should explain before we go any further, Mr Perrett, it can only be a temporary arrangement, my working here I mean, just until you can get something else fixed up ... I have ... ' she hesitated, feeling his quick, penetrating glance, 'I have other commitments. I can really only manage a month at the most. Meantime I suggest you get in touch with some agencies right away ... '

He gulped back the neat spirit in one swallow.

'That's O.K., lass. At least it'll give me a chance to look around for someone permanent, and to get top-sides with some of this bumf.' He swept his hand in the direction of the desk, which was piled with heaps of papers, letters, forms and account books.

'So long as I know someone compe-tent and reliable's out there, keeping the customers happy, and the staff under control, then that suits me, and I reckon you can do all that to a tee. Now,' he rubbed his hands together, 'first off let's get the name business right. I'd rather you called me Sam, more friendly like, and what's your first name?'

Margaret looked directly at him, shaking her head slowly, a half smile on her lips as if to soften the words she uttered, 'Now there you go again, it won't do, you really must learn not to mix business and pleasure . . . '

She felt her face burn as he frowned quickly, and she remembered the scene she had witnessed only the night before between him and the manageress — maybe she should have sugared the pill a little more . . . 'I mean — I think it's better to keep things on a formal basis, anyway to start with.'

He shrugged his shoulders, slightly mollified by her tone.

'O.K., if that's the way you want it, it's Mrs Smith and Mr Perrett then.

And I take it you're a widow, or divorced, so that there isn't any likelihood of a Mr Smith coming chasing after you — if that's the right name, which I doubt,' he added slyly.

But Margaret wasn't going to be caught. She dropped her eyes for lies didn't come easily, but she had no intention of letting Sam into her private life at this stage.

'I am alone shall we say — not that I see it really matters, it will have no bearing on my work here — my private life,' she smiled at him again.

'Right. The only reason I ask is insurance cards — have you had a job before?'

She hadn't thought of that, hadn't realised all the complications in which her impetuous action was going to involve her . . .

She shook her head. 'Not exactly, at least I've not been 'gainfully employed' as I believe they put it. I have done a kind of housekeeping job, but I wasn't paid an official salary so I didn't have

61

any cards — does that make things difficult?'

Privately Sam made a shrewd guess at what she meant, although she didn't strike him as that type of woman, and it seemed very odd she should have turned up in an out of the way place like Queensbridge in what he recognised as very expensive clothes, with expensive luggage, and a genuine diamond solitaire ring on her finger — and as an associate or whatever, of a man like John Beckett — who he could smell as ex-fuzz a mile off . . . still it was really none of his business . . . as long as the police weren't looking for her, and he doubted that, she had a kind of transparent innocence that couldn't have been assumed . . .

He ran his fingers through his short, coarse hair so that it stood on end like broom bristles, a gesture which Margaret found endearing, giving her a sudden longing to put out her hand and smooth it down again.

'Oh I've no doubt there's some form

'N' or something or other we can fill in to keep the Social Security people happy — I like things on the up and up, no hanky panky with the Income Tax or anything of that sort — you understand? Life's full enough of difficulties without us making any more . . . '

She nodded and got to her feet. 'Well, the sooner I start my duties the better, and I must move my things. I take it there are some rooms for the staff to sleep in?'

'There won't be any need for that,' he said sharply, 'we don't have that many residents queuing up that we can't spare our manageress a nice room.'

Margaret thought briefly of the room she'd spent the night in. She would hardly have classified that as 'nice', but she supposed it was probably about the best the hotel had to offer.

'How many of the staff do live in?'

'Only the manageress. The rest are local — apart from cook, and she has a flat in the town. The girl Teresa is in digs I suppose, she came down from the

Midlands, old Joe and his wife have a terraced house down the bottom of the town, the two girls in the kitchen, and Vi in the bar, all live around somewhere,' he said vaguely.

'But there must be staff rooms in the attic,' she persisted, 'I don't want any special treatment. I'll look into it . . . '

She climbed the narrow stairs from the landing where her own bedroom had been and found two small rooms under the roof.

They were dingy in the extreme with tiny dormer windows, and damp patches on the low ceilings where the rain had soaked through. Boiling hot in summer, and freezing in winter, she thought. The wallpaper was peeling in several places, and the furniture rickety and dusty — her heart sank as she looked round. But she had chosen to work here, and she fully intended to carry out her plan to the letter, anyway it all reminded her vividly of the pub she had been brought up in . . .

Going back to her bedroom she saw

that the door to the room next to it was open. Evidently the manageress had packed in double quick time as it was empty, the bed unmade and pieces of tissues, cotton wool and patches of face powder covered the dressing table. Margaret was relieved the woman had actually gone, she had feared some kind of confrontation — she recognised the type and dreaded a showdown which she was sure would have had fishwife overtones at the least.

As she went into her own room to put her few belongings into her case, Teresa came slowly along the landing, clean sheets and pillow-cases over her arm. Margaret supposed Sam had told her to make up a fresh bed for the new manageress.

'Hullo, are those for me?' she asked brightly. The girl nodded, still without speaking. Margaret suppressed an impatient longing to give her a gentle shake and ask teasingly 'Cat got your tongue, love?' But she said, 'Then I'll give you a hand.'

She followed the still silent girl up the attic stairs and started to help her make up the bed.

'I hope we're going to be friends now, Teresa. Shall I help you tidy up the two rooms that are empty? I daresay at this time of year they'll be needed right away.'

The girl shrugged her shoulders, and then for the first time Margaret heard her daughter's voice. It was surprisingly low and musical, quite out of keeping with her appearance, and she was so busy listening to its tone that she didn't take in what she said.

Suddenly she realised some kind of reply was expected, but as if she were used to having her questions unanswered, the girl turned and walked out of the room before Margaret could regain her composure sufficiently to ask her what she had said.

She looked once more round the uncomfortable room, thinking for a moment of the luxury of her own bedroom at home with its roomy bed, its shaded lights and adjoining bath-room.

But she must be prepared to sacrifice her comfort at least in the realisation of the dream she had dreamed with increasing intensity for so many years.

The thought of home brought her up sharply — she would have to go out to a phone box and ring Muriel Grailey, tell her she was staying on and give her the phone number, impressing upon her the fact that she was not to ring under any circumstances unless it was literally a matter of life or death . . .

Meanwhile Sam sat in his office, smoking a cigar. He found the whole situation both odd and intensely intriguing, but he had the good sense to decide to say nothing, to pursue it no further at the moment. His north country shrewdness had taught him not to look a gift horse in the mouth, and he was astute enough to realise he had found a jewel in Margaret, experience or no, she had the *savoir-faire* — the 'nous' as he described it to himself

— to impress the customers. Apart from commonsense, she had tact — he admired in others what he lacked in himself.

When he explained to her briefly what the job entailed, she thought how remarkably simple it was compared with the complicated business of running a big house, bringing up two kids, and entertaining Hugh's business associates — with no half days off.

Mainly her job would be to deal with bookings — if any — answer the phone, supervise the staff and dining room, go through the menus with the cook, and order the food . . .

The staff consisted of the porter cum waiter — Joe, the cook, and two girls known as stillroom maids, but who, in spite of the rather grand title, just did all the odd jobs round the kitchen — and then of course there was Teresa . . .

Margaret would dearly have liked to pension off the waiter, or put a rocket behind him, she thought ruefully, but after having a chat with him she realised he wasn't all that old — just unenthusiastic, and she guessed he drank more than he should when on duty . . . she decided that somehow, tactfully, she would edge him out of the dining room and put Teresa in his place as waitress . . .

There was a brassy girl by the name of Vi, in the bar . . . after spending one evening watching her, Margaret realised she was putting off more customers than she attracted — and attracting the wrong sort at that. Her manner was all wrong, too familiar and brash — and after all I ought to know, she thought ruefully.

Tactfully she tried to explain to Sam. 'She'd be fine in a city pub, or a four ale bar, but this is a market town, a country area, most of the people who come in here for a drink are farmers and their wives, families out for the evening who don't want to go just into a cider bar. I think Joe would be excellent behind the bar, he'd go down well with those kind of customers. He's well known in the town too, a local, not a 'furriner' like Vi. And you've only got one other pub to compete with from what I hear, you could make quite a thing out of the bar, after all this is a very old pub and full of character . . . '

'Hey, lass, you haven't taken long to find all that out . . . ' he said, grinning, 'reckon you'll know more about the business than I do by tomorrow . . . do whatever you think . . . '

Joe took to the bar like duck to water. Word soon went round that Vi had been replaced, and with the fickleness of the general public, they came from the other pub.

Margaret knew she was taking a gamble over the drink problem for now Joe would have it close to hand all the time, but the odd part was, much as she had suspected, he took on a new lease of life and didn't drink as much as he had — in fact now a couple of pints lasted him through the evening.

She mentioned it to Sam. 'I think he

felt frustrated in the other job, missed the company or something. He gets on much better in a casual atmosphere, and up to now he's been so busy, he hasn't much time to drink himself.'

Next she spent a whole afternoon going through the linen cupboard.

It was obvious no woman had tackled it for years. She wondered briefly how long Sam had actually had the Pack Horse.

She threw out the darned and threadbare sheets for dusters, the stained table cloths and napkins could be boiled and used as dish cloths. She told Sam she was going to buy fresh linen at the local drapers, and gaily coloured plastic table mats for the dining room.

When she'd whipped the dirty cloths off the tables she discovered they were good solid oak, only in need of a wipe over with some vinegar and a good polish.

She unearthed some little glass finger bowls and filled them with summer flowers, so that the dining room began to look cheerful and friendly instead of grey and forbidding.

'Lass, you've done a grand job, things are looking up already,' Sam rubbed his hands. Margaret smiled, she hadn't enjoyed herself so much for years. It was the challenge that answered something that had been lacking in her life up to now.

At least that was the explanation she gave herself . . .

4

Sam liked his own kind about him, and the Yorkshire cook was good at her job — as far as it went. Good solid plain food — she hadn't got round to what she described as 'fancy bits' — prawn cocktails and sea food salads . . .

Margaret offered to do them, tactfully adding she could see Mrs Lewis had quite enough to do without messing about with such frills, but in these days of foreign holidays, people brought back these ideas from abroad with them, seemed to expect them — specially the younger generation.

One afternoon she got Sam to put on an old pair of slacks and shirt and together they painted the tubs in front of the hotel a bright blue, and filled them with scarlet geraniums.

'There's nothing much we can do about the paintwork on the outside, I

73

realise that,' she said, 'but at least the windows can be clean and shining, and the curtains freshly washed and starched, so that it looks as though someone lives here — and cares . . . '

It was incredible how much she achieved in just a few days, Sam thought. One afternoon as she stood at the reception desk he came out of the office, and watched her entering up a fresh batch of bookings which had come in the post.

He put his arm lightly along her shoulders.

'Lass, I wouldn't have believed it possible a few licks of paint, a dash of soap and water, and a switch around of staff could make such a difference.'

The warmth of his arm against the back of her neck sent a little shiver of excitement down her spine.

Then she remembered she'd seen him one evening with his arm round the cook when he wanted to cajole her into some special dish . . . she was about to draw away, but somehow she told herself, this was different, she could tell, there was a look of respect in his eyes. It wasn't just the familiar kind of casual embrace a man like Sam would take for granted with his staff . . .

Smiling, she turned to face him. 'Maybe, but we've only scratched the surface. There's lots more needs doing. The furniture in the lounge for instance, the covers are a disgrace, and two of the chairs need re-upholstering. You should put a new carpet in the hall and on the stairs, first impressions are important — and apart from the paintwork on the outside, it needs a coat of Snowcem on the walls . . .'

'Steady on lass, I'm not made of brass thou knows!'

'I know, but you have to speculate to accumulate my husband always says . . .'

Too late she realised she'd used the present tense . . .

His eyes met and held hers a moment . . . 'I mean — used to say. Sometimes I forget.'

She turned away and then quickly changed the subject before he could ask any questions . . . 'And while I think of it, are you trying to find someone to take on this job? You must remember I'm only temporary . . . '

He leant against the counter, his arms folded.

'I know you said as much. But you do like it here don't you? Enjoy the work I mean. Things are going to improve in the west country with the new motorway and all. Place'll be knee deep in holidaymakers, just like the east coast. If we go on improving this place like you've started to do, I could offer you . . . ' he paused, not looking at her now. Margaret's heart pounded in her ears . . . 'I'd like to make you some kind of partner,' he finished lamely, and she knew it wasn't what he'd started out to say . . .

She shook her head. 'I'm afraid that's impossible, although naturally I'm flattered by your suggestion, but I told you at the start, I can only stay a little while.'

She bent over the register so he shouldn't see her face . . . 'There are other things I have to do . . . '

In the meantime she felt the whole purpose of the decision she had made to stay on at the Pack Horse, to get to know and help Teresa — was not making much progress.

One afternoon when she'd been out shopping for odds and ends for the hotel, she'd met her in the main street. It had been something of a shock when she saw her, for she was wandering along, arms entwined, with what Margaret could only describe to herself as a 'creature'. She knew Hippies as such were out of date, but this must be one left over from the craze, she thought.

He had bare feet, his jeans appeared to be stiff with grease, dirt and paint, he had on an old tee shirt whose original colour had disappeared under a layer of more splashes of paint, and his hair hung in lank, greasy ringlets, mingling with a half-grown beard and sideburns.

For a moment the sight of him filled Margaret with such revulsion it was almost like a physical sickness . . . but she made herself stop Teresa . . . 'Hullo, I was just going to have a cup of tea. Would you like to join me?'

Before the girl could answer, the boy said, 'Why not? So long as you're paying. I could do with some nosh, Terry.'

The girl pulled on his arm, trying to get away, her cheeks flushed, she looked more surly and sulky than ever . . .

Oh dear, Margaret thought, I've done the wrong thing again. The poor child didn't want me to meet him, and she just hasn't any confidence in herself . . .

But obviously the idea of a free meal appealed more to the boy than whatever Teresa's wishes might be . . .

Margaret felt hot with embarrassment as they went into the café, and wished they'd been outside the self service food bar, which had just opened at the top of the town, when they met, instead of the Tudor Rose.

It was one of those rather exclusive places run by two spinster ladies who made all their own cakes. The one who came to take their order looked from Margaret to the boy with undisguised amazement and disbelief . . .

Margaret gave her what she hoped was a reassuring smile and sat down, drawing off her gloves. As she did so she saw the boy glance swiftly under his lashes at her diamond ring . . .

She held out the menu. 'What would you like to eat?'

He ran a dirty finger down the list.

She turned to Teresa. 'Perhaps you'd introduce us, I don't even know your friend's name.'

'You can call me Tad,' he said quickly, 'wot's in a name I always say, and that's what most people call me, short for Tadpole — I was called that at the Orphanage,' he added, sniggering, 'mostly because I was better at catching them than the others . . .'

'Well it's unusual,' she said brightly, trying to put Teresa at her ease, and break some of the ice.

She tried to remember if Mike had had a surly streak . . . she thought bitterly that she hadn't really known him all that long, and not all that well — and had been too blinded by the passion she felt for him to notice any defects . . . maybe with Teresa it was just a kind of defence mechanism, a shell of protection she'd built up in the Orphanage, the fact that she'd never belonged anywhere — that no one really cared . . . maybe this too could account for the dreadful companion she had chosen. Up to now she really couldn't see anything to recommend him . . .

It was as if he'd never had a square meal before. He wolfed down the elegantly served plaice and chips, smothering them with sauce, a plate of bread and butter — mopping up the grease with his fingers. Then he had a banana-split and four iced cakes

. . . Margaret felt sure if she'd suggested he go through the whole programme again, he would have done so with the greatest ease.

Meanwhile Teresa sat silent, sipping a cup of tea, shaking her head when Margaret offered her a cake. She seemed almost hypnotised by Tad as she watched him demolishing the food.

Margaret tried to draw her out by talking about the changes she'd made at the hotel.

'Are you enjoying working in the dining room?'

The girl nodded, showing a spark of interest at last. 'Yes, thank you.'

'I'm always there to help if you're in any difficulty, you know.'

She nodded, but her eyes swung back to Tad, who was noisily draining his fifth cup of tea. Then she said defensively, as though Margaret might be silently criticising his behaviour.

'Tad doesn't have much time to get his meals, he's an artist, does murals and things . . . '

At least that accounted for the paint splashes — Margaret tried to look interested. 'That's nice. What are you working on at the moment?' she looked at Tad.

He shook his head. 'Nowt. I was going to do one in the new Caf up the top of the town, but they got in some oick with short back and sides from London, didn't like my ideas, said they were too way out . . . bloody idiots . . . '

Margaret could imagine what his designs might be like, but she merely said, 'What a shame, still I expect there are other places . . . '

He shrugged. 'Maybe — it's a dump though — maybe all right for some, not for the true artist though.' He emptied the sugar basin into his pocket. Margaret prayed the lady who served them hadn't noticed . . .

There was silence for a moment as she tried desperately to think of something to say.

'Tad shares a caravan at Hope's Bay,' Teresa went on, as though he were a small child who had to be talked for . . .

'That should be nice,' Margaret said, glancing at her watch.

'It isn't so, it's another dump,' Tad said with surprising heat . . .

'I really must get back, some new residents are arriving this afternoon.' Margaret got to her feet and paid the bill, leaving a large tip under her plate, hoping it would cover the cost of the sugar, but she had a distinct feeling Tad, who was now emptying the milk jug into his cup — would probably remove it as soon as her back was turned . . .

She left them sitting without speaking at the table, resisting with great difficulty the temptation to glance back through the window when she got into the street.

She went up the steps into the hotel with a heavy cloud of depression pressing about her.

How on earth was she ever going to help the girl, make any lasting impression in such a short time.

The task seemed more hopeless than ever now she had met who was obviously her choice of boy friend . . .

★ ★ ★

She had ordered some bright cotton dresses and aprons from the drapers when she'd bought the new linen, and now she asked Teresa to choose what she would like to wear as she worked in the dining room.

For a moment, as her eyes brightened, she looked almost pretty . . . She chose a yellow dress with a light brown apron, and another in apple green with pink. Margaret held the dresses up against her, the colours suited her, brought the pale complexion to life . . .

'I've got a lipstick upstairs that would just go with these. It's not my colour at all, much more yours. Can't think really what made me buy it . . . I'll fetch it.'

Teresa accepted it with a ghost of a smile and a little more grace than she usually showed.

'Can you tell me the best hairdresser in town?' Margaret went on, anxious to press home any small advance she might have made by being friendly.

Teresa shook her head. 'Don't know, I can't afford to go myself.'

It sounded like a snub, the kind of thing Tad would have said, but whether she really meant it as such Margaret couldn't be sure . . .

'How about letting me treat you — to celebrate the new job? We'll try that one next to the new café at the top of the town, at least it looks bright and clean.'

The girl shrugged her shoulders. 'I don't mind. If you like.' Her voice was colourless, expressionless and once more Margaret felt a burning desire to give her a little shake into some kind of animation at least.

However she did allow the girl in the salon to cut her rather heavy, lank hair, and give it a light perm and comb it into soft curls round her face.

It made all the difference, and Margaret watched her as she looked at the new image in the mirror. For a moment her lips parted, her eyes shone, even her skin seemed to have a new, inner radiance.

She could be quite beautiful, Margaret thought, with a little catch in her throat. Maybe this is the beginning of a breakthrough — maybe soon I will find what is underneath these protective layers, help to give her some self confidence at least . . .

The dining room was fully booked for dinner most evenings now, and Teresa had her hands full.

She was deft and quick at waiting. To begin with she had a little difficulty in sorting out who ordered what, in spite of the notebook in which she wrote down the orders, but Margaret hovered like a kind of guardian angel near the door, watching discreetly, ready to help but overjoyed that most of the time it wasn't necessary, and that the girl really did seem to be making an effort.

Suddenly as she glanced round the room she saw the woman who was sitting alone at a window table.

Her heart did a somersault.

Sybil Seymour! Of all people. She had been a fellow member of the flower-arranging class Margaret had joined at home. What rotten luck. It was something she hadn't bargained for. After all she was a good three hours journey away from home, and in an ordinary and somewhat remote market town in the heart of Devon — there was virtually nothing to attract outsiders, except the races at Bushel, and they were over for the time being . . .

As she stood rooted to the spot as if an evil dream, the woman got up and came to the door, obviously looking for something or someone.

Before Margaret could turn away, she caught her arm, 'Excuse me, could you tell me . . . ,' she stopped abruptly. 'Good heavens, Margaret Gennert! I'm so sorry, I thought for a moment you were on the staff — what on earth are you doing in a dump like this? I shouldn't be here myself if the car hadn't broken down ... anyway I thought you were in America with Hugh ... '

The whole dining room seemed to have turned their eyes on Sybil and herself as they stood there. She had one of those penetrating voices that reached the furthermost table ... Margaret prayed Sam was out of earshot, and thanked heaven Teresa herself had just gone through the service door to the kitchen quarters.

She looked Sybil straight in the eye without flinching. 'I'm sorry, I'm afraid you've made a mistake, my name is Smith and I am employed here, Madam. The cloakroom, if that was what you wanted, is on the first floor, the second door on the left. Excuse me, I have things to attend to in the office ... '

She turned swiftly and went through the first door she came to, her mind in a turmoil.

To her intense relief the woman made no attempt to follow her, although she could hear her mutter, 'Well honestly, I could have sworn . . . must be her double . . . '

The door Margaret had gone through happened to be the office, and in her haste she nearly knocked Sam over. He gave her a quick look, for actually he had seen the whole occurrence through the glass panel, and his curiosity about his efficient manageress was even more aroused . . .

Ever since she'd taken the job he'd been watching her intently. He was deeply attracted to her as a woman, but there was so much about her he didn't understand, so much that didn't add up — that made him wonder.

Maybe this enigma was part of the attraction, most women had little mystery these days, and more's the pity, he thought.

Now Margaret went over to the desk and pretended to be looking for some old menus to try and hide her confusion. She bent forward with the light behind her profile, which threw the tip-tilted nose and the rather full mouth, into perspective.

She lifted her hand to push the hair back from her face — and suddenly, sharply he was reminded of someone else ... it was an elusive, teasing memory of a face which he tried to capture, to pin down — but still it eluded him ...

'Can I help you find whatever it is you're looking for?' he asked, his hand on her arm so that once again she felt that electric thrill along her nerves. It made her jump for she'd been preoccupied with the encounter she'd had with Sybil, and shocked too, more than she liked to admit. She had begun to feel a complacency, sure she was safe in this backwater, and the meeting had disturbed her equilibrium. She didn't know Sybil all that well, but somehow she had the feeling she would be the kind of woman who delighted in gossiping ...

As if he sensed her unease, and the fact that she was upset and needed comforting, Sam bent and kissed her gently on the cheek . . .

'Don't worry Maggie love, it may never happen,' he whispered in her ear.

For a moment she felt surprise tinged with annoyance at the kiss . . . she stood as if turned to stone. The surprise wasn't at the fact that Sam had kissed her, she would not have been a woman if she hadn't realised he was attracted to her — it was at the rush of her own emotion — a warmth and desire she had forgotten existed — and the sudden knowledge that she herself could easily fall in love with him.

He'd never called her Maggie before — not even Margaret in respect of her wishes. No one had ever called her Maggie . . . now her annoyance dissolved and she wanted to laugh . . . she liked it — it was warm, human, intimate, giving her a sense of belonging, of being needed that she hadn't experienced for a long time . . . not since those early, carefree days with Mike perhaps . . .

She lifted her fingers to touch the spot he had kissed . . .

But when she turned to speak to him he had gone . . .

★　★　★

Although she was unaccustomed to being on her feet all day, and working so hard, that night Margaret couldn't get to sleep.

It had been after midnight when she eventually got to bed, and she was half listening for Teresa's step on the stairs, for she had suggested to Sam that the girl have the little room next to hers to sleep in.

He had looked at her quizzically, and quickly, to allay any suspicions he might have she said, 'It'll save her money, heaven knows you don't pay her much.' She didn't add that it meant too she could keep an eye on her and see she had three good meals a day. She was painfully thin and needed feeding up . . . Margaret felt Sam could easily afford those meals — although she didn't tell him so.

Also she didn't trust Tad. He looked as if he smoked pot at the very least, she thought grimly, possibly something worse, and if Teresa slept under the same roof as herself at least she would have some idea of what she was up to.

Much to her surprise, the girl had agreed quite willingly, and moved her few possessions in the next day. Usually she went out when she'd finished serving dinners, but came home before midnight when Sam locked up.

The hotel was too small to justify a night porter, and now Joe worked in the bar, they had an odd job man who helped with the luggage, cleaned the shoes and so on, but he went off after dinner when any new guest had usually arrived and settled in.

Now Margaret's mind was active, and there seemed to be more traffic than usual grinding up the steep hill, she was uneasy still too, about the encounter with Sybil Seymour.

But she was on the threshold of sleep when she heard voices downstairs . . .

She raised herself on her elbow and switched on the light.

Probably some of the guests were keeping Sam up. She could hear his gruff Yorkshire tones — and a woman's voice.

For a moment she wondered if the manageress had come back to make trouble . . . she had gone off eventually in a remarkably docile frame of mind, not what Margaret had anticipated at all . . .

But as she listened she realised this was a softer voice, not the harsh tones she'd used . . .

Suddenly she realised it was Teresa . . . and it sounded as if they were having a row . . .

Wide awake now she threw on her dressing gown and slippers and started down the stairs.

They were standing in the office with the door open and she could hear Sam's voice clearly now . . .

'I might have known a girl who'd had the number of jobs you have must be a misfit, or even worse. Wouldn't surprise me if half those references you brought me you'd written yourself . . . '

The girl made some reply which was inaudible to Margaret, but she was suddenly suffused with an unreasoning fury at Sam, a primitive, maternal instinct to protect her young, making the blood pound in her pulses, and she knew she could easily strike out at him in her anger — give the whole game away if she didn't gain control of herself . . .

'Trouble with Orphanage kids you got no idea what sort of stock they come from, but I was willing to give you a chance, I never thought you'd repay me like this . . . '

Margaret paused a moment, trying to calm her nerves . . . then she went on down the stairs, her slippers making no sound on the carpet.

Now, nearer, she could hear Teresa . . . 'It isn't you who've been so good, it's Mrs Smith . . . ' her tone was defiant, held more spirit than Margaret had ever heard her use.

'I'm well aware of that, and a nice way you've chosen to repay such a lady,' he replied hotly.

Margaret had reached them now. The girl's face was flushed and sulky. Sam had an open cash box and a handful of dining room checks in his hand. He swung round as he heard her step on the hall floor.

'What the . . . ? Oh, it's you . . . a nice kettle of fish we've got on our hands here, gratitude for doing anyone a good turn this is . . . biting the hand that fed her,' he ended dramatically. His Yorkshire accent was thicker than Margaret had ever heard it, and he seemed to bristle all over, like a porcupine . . . in spite of her anger, for a moment she had a ridiculous desire to laugh . . .

The girl didn't raise her head as Margaret came towards them. She merely pulled with shaking fingers at a loose thread in her skirt . . .

Margaret went to her and put her arm round her. She could feel her whole body trembling and some of her anger returned, but as she lifted her head, her eyes were defiant and she tried to pull away from Margaret's firm grasp.

It was then, as they stood side by side in front of him like two wild creatures at bay, that suddenly Sam knew who it was Margaret had reminded him of earlier in the day — Teresa . . .

The colouring was different, but the bone structure, the nose, and the shape of the teeth — so often an hereditary feature — they were all there . . .

He knew without a shadow of doubt that mother and daughter stood before him . . .

But for the moment that piece of information did not interest him at all . . .

'What exactly is the trouble?' Margaret's voice was full of chips of ice . . .

'You may well ask.' He blustered

slightly, somewhat intimidated by her presence, and by the look on her face — however he was determined to press on — two women weren't going to frighten Sam Perrett . . . 'There's five pounds missing from the dining room takings, and only one who handles the cash — her!'

He pointed at Teresa . . .

5

Margaret's heart seemed to miss a beat as she stared at Sam's accusing finger. She gave him a long cool look, the fierce protectiveness she felt for Teresa surged through her, she said very slowly and distinctly, 'I also handle the cash from the dining room.'

For a moment Sam looked at her in astonishment, then he exploded, 'Don't be damned silly, it's obvious you wouldn't take a fiver!'

'Why? You know nothing about me and I've worked here a much shorter time than Teresa. I think you're simply jumping to conclusions on circumstantial evidence . . .'

Sam was thrown for words, he looked flustered, then he said, 'Well, I was going through the cash in the dining room till, checking it against the slips — there's definitely five pounds missing — and that's only one day's takings — heaven knows how much more's gone. And Miss here says she knows nothing about it . . . '

'Teresa brings me the cash in the box at the end of each meal, I don't usually have time to check it against all the bills at once, but they are put directly into the safe, no one else handles them.'

Sam subsided like a pricked balloon. Margaret felt a momentary stab of pity for him. He looked lonely and vulnerable standing there, not quite knowing how to handle the situation . . .

'That's utterly ridiculous — I mean I know you couldn't . . . wouldn't . . . ' His voice petered out as she glared at him.

'How do you know?' she asked coolly, 'as I just told you, you know nothing about me, less than you know about Teresa. I came with no references at all — not even any insurance cards.'

She was determined to twist the knife, whatever sympathy she might have for Sam . . .

'Yes . . . but . . . ' he said weakly, all the fight gone out of him now . . .

'So shall we go into the office and discuss this thing properly and sanely without losing our tempers and saying things we shall all regret later?'

She fully intended to press home her advantage.

Now the girl looked at Margaret, her mouth sulky, but there was something else in her expression which her mother couldn't quite define — fear perhaps, or even faint horror. All the life seemed to have gone out of her, just as it had with Sam — even her hair looked dull . . .

'I . . . ' her voice was hardly above a whisper . . . 'could I have a word with you alone, Mrs Smith?' Her eyes were pleading now.

Sam looked annoyed again, but before he could burst out with some other explosive, Margaret said quickly, 'Yes, of course, come into the dining room a moment, then we shan't disturb any guests who are trying to sleep . . . '

She closed the door softly behind

her. The girl seemed to be a bag of nerves.

'Now anything you tell me will be in the strictest confidence, I promise you that Teresa.'

The girl nodded. 'Yes, I know,' she hesitated a moment, then she said in a rush, 'You know the boy I was with the other day — Tad — you very kindly gave us tea . . . '

Margaret nodded, she wasn't likely to forget.

'Well . . . I mean there may be nothing in it — like you said just now, circumstantial evidence — and heaven knows I'd be the last to jump to conclusions I hope, or give a dog a bad name and hang it . . . I've had all that happen to me too often — but he did call in the other day at lunch time to arrange about seeing me in the evening. It was Wednesday, Market Day, and I was very busy in the dining room . . . ' she hesitated.

Margaret nodded encouragingly, 'Yes, I remember. I was annoyed because I snagged my tights on the edge of the desk, they were a new pair, and I had to dash upstairs to change them. Is that when you mean?'

'Yes. You see Tad came in directly you'd gone up the stairs, almost as if he'd been watching . . . at the time I thought perhaps he didn't want you to see him in case you were annoyed at him hanging about the hotel — now I'm — wondering . . . you see the cash box stands just inside the door here,' she pointed to the service table where rows of cutlery and glasses were laid out.

Her voice dropped to a whisper again, she twisted her hands together nervously . . . 'I suppose it would be dead easy for anyone to slip their hand in there . . . ' she paused again and Margaret waited for her to finish. 'I don't really know how long he'd been standing there — but surely it couldn't really be him, not after . . . I hate saying this, hate thinking it even . . . but it wasn't me, I swear that . . . '

Margaret put her arm round her. 'We're going to have to handle this very tactfully, Teresa. I know you didn't take it because you tell me so — but we don't want to accuse Tad unless we're absolutely certain, and the point is if he could have done it, I suppose so could a dozen other people really . . . it's a very tricky situation.' She hesitated a moment, then she said, 'I know it's nothing to do with me, but how well do you know him? It would be a help if you could tell me a few details about him . . .'

The girl swallowed, 'Yes I suppose so. I haven't really known him very long. I met him in the coffee bar, you know, the new one at the top of the street. I used to go there sometimes for a cheap meal when I had the bed sitter, before I got meals in the hotel,' she gave a half smile . . . 'anyway it was when he thought he might get the job of doing the mural, and we got talking. I soon found out he was lonely like me.

'We seemed to have quite a lot in

common in fact, neither of us knew who our parents had been. He'd been fostered from a baby — luckier than me in a way because at least he had some kind of home . . . anyway it made a kind of bond between us . . . ' she paused again and Margaret felt a stab of pain at the pathetic words, 'at least he had some kind of home . . . '

Teresa went on, 'Actually I'd only been out with him a few times, I'd never been back to the caravan where he lives or anything like that. But I did think we were friends, I didn't think he'd do anything like this to me, after all he might know I'd be accused . . . ' For a moment there was a touch of defiance in the darkness of her eyes. She looked straight at Margaret . . .

She put out her hand and touched the girl's hand.

'I'm certain you meant well, Teresa, and we may of course be wrong about Tad. Anyway I'll see what I can do with Mr Perrett, try to persuade him it'll be best to keep the hotel out of the papers by not going to the police . . . ' She hesitated, 'Are you seeing Tad again soon?'

Teresa nodded. 'The day after tomorrow actually. He's got to go down to Plymouth tomorrow on some kind of business or other. Do you want me to ask him — about the money I mean?'

'Well,' Margaret said slowly, 'I suppose it would be better than putting the police straight on him as I said, specially if he's innocent, it might make him even more resentful and unhappy if he thinks we're all against him — which we aren't . . . '

Teresa nodded, 'I'm so glad you say that — I wish everyone felt the same. But I'll have to be very careful, tactful, won't I?'

Margaret nodded. 'I'm sure you can handle it, and for the time being I'll make the money right with Mr Perrett, and persuade him to let it ride for a day or two, then you see if in some roundabout way you can find out from Tad . . . what do you say? Maybe if he seems to be flashing his money about more than usual — that kind of thing . . . '

The girl looked at her again, 'If only they were all as kind as you,' she said softly. Then to Margaret's utter amazement she suddenly flung her arms round her and kissed her.

She was so shaken that for a moment she couldn't speak, couldn't react. Then she said, 'Well thank you, but I don't know that I've done anything much to deserve it . . . '

'For the moment it was almost as if you . . . as if I had a mother of my own who really cared, it's the way normal mothers behave to their daughters — not like mine did, just going off and leaving me . . . she must have been the most unnatural woman that ever lived . . . not a bit like you . . . '

Before Margaret could recover from the shock, or fully absorb all that the girl had just said to her, she had turned and dashed from the room and up the stairs . . .

She longed to go after her, but restrained herself. At least there was a ray of hope now, perhaps at last she was making some kind of breakthrough . . . the kiss had been more like a child would give a grown up — soft as a moth's wing on her cheek.

She turned off the dining room light and went across to Sam's office, squaring her shoulders as she tried to decide what argument to use to convince him of Teresa's innocence, and persuade him not to call in the police yet.

He was banging books about and sifting through papers on his desk. 'I don't know what's with the young people these days, always thinking the world owes them a living. Pity they don't have the good sense to appreciate what's done for them. When I was young . . .'

'We don't need to go into your past history at this precise moment,' Margaret said, more sharply than she intended, half scared that the showdown might end in Teresa getting the sack . . . 'and I'm quite convinced after talking to her that the girl is innocent . . . '

'Well I'm not,' his tone matched hers as he reached out to the phone. 'I'm going to get the cops on it anyway.'

Margaret quickly put out her hand to stop him.

'I wouldn't do that if I were you. After all there's no great harm done. I'll make up the money. I'm responsible for the staff and also for the money collected for meals in the dining room. I should have kept my eyes open . . . it shows I have a lot to learn . . . and bringing in the police will only put the hotel in a bad light. Guests don't like that kind of thing . . . '

Sam stood looking at her for a full minute. Her eyes met his — level and unwavering. His head was hunched into his shoulders so he looked more than ever like a bull terrier.

At last his glance fell before hers. She sighed with relief. And suddenly she felt a surge of gratitude to this strange little man . . . He spoke more quietly now.

'I'm making no promises, but from now on all the cash from the dining room will have to be brought direct to the office.'

'I quite understand, I think that a very good idea — and in the meantime will you leave the tracing of the thief to me? I haven't any direct information, but I do have a lead, something Teresa told me in confidence. But it's no good going at it bull in a china shop, just let me do it my way, and then if by the end of the week I've had no luck, then we shall have to call in the police.'

Sam turned on his heel. 'You're soft in the head as well as the heart.'

He paused a moment. Then swung round again, looking directly at her, 'But she's your lass, isn't she?'

Margaret was caught off guard and the word 'Yes' slipped out before she had time to think. She felt the hot colour flood her face, then she said, 'Yes, she's my daughter, but she doesn't

110

know it, and she is never to find out, I'd like to make that absolutely clear,' her eyes flashed a warning at him and her chin lifted defiantly.

Sam thought what a magnificent woman she was when she was angry.

Suddenly, to her amazement, he burst out laughing, all his anger dissolved by the look, the nearness of her . . .

'Keep your cool as they say, Maggie love. I won't give away your little secret. Reckon most of us have some kind of skeleton rattling its bones in the cupboard if the truth's known, and I like a woman with spirit and character . . . and with a bit of mystery in her background, not wishy washy like some . . . '

Suddenly all the tension that had been building up in Margaret burst and she sat down in the chair by the desk, and putting her head down on her hands, started to cry.

Sam let her sob for a moment while he fetched a drink from the cupboard.

'Here you are, lass, drink that down and dry your eyes with this.' He passed her a handkerchief which smelt faintly of good, old fashioned cologne and cigar smoke. 'Do you good to get it out of your system. I knew there was something when a woman like you took on a job like this. I'm not so green as cabbage looking, as they say . . . '

Margaret had to smile through her tears. 'I never would have suggested such a thing where you are concerned.'

He put his hand on her shoulder. 'Had a hard life, the kid, I reckon, made her a bit prickly. You're not going to have an easy job there, whatever you do. Think it best to keep your true identity from her, do you?'

She nodded. 'Yes, I suppose it's silly, but I couldn't bear her to know who I am — I just want to help her, try to make up a little for what I did — do all I can for her . . . '

'Yes, I can see that. She's mixed with the wrong crowd I expect, they get kind of hang ups, these kids from Homes and Orphanages sometimes . . . '

'I'll never be able to forgive myself for letting her be put in an Orphanage — but it's difficult to explain to the young today the reasons we did things — it was so different twenty years ago — even ten. Subjects never mentioned then are just common talk today. If it had happened today I suppose I wouldn't have thought twice about keeping her, bringing her up myself, like so many girls do.'

'Father not want to marry you?' Sam asked shortly, not really wanting to probe, but fascinated more than he liked to admit, by this woman.

She shook her head. 'No, he just didn't want to know when I told him I was pregnant, in fact he disappeared, left his job with no forwarding address or anything. My mother sent me away, up to the Midlands to an aunt. She took the baby to an Orphanage. Mike, Teresa's father — had been lodging in our pub . . . ' she paused. 'I was only seventeen, and in those days quite a lot of us of that age simply didn't know how many beans made five, had no idea what life and love and sex was all about . . . '

'Never been married myself,' Sam said, sipping his drink, 'reckon it has its advantages as well as its drawbacks,' he chuckled. 'That woman — the one who left, Miss Hoity Toity I called her — she thought she was on a good thing with me — catch of the season I was — and I fell for it to a certain extent. Trouble is I'm lonely I suppose,' he was half talking to himself . . .

Margaret had an almost overwhelming desire to confide further in him, to tell him about Hugh, about her home and Linda and Tim . . . but she fought it down. She didn't want to commit herself, to become too involved . . . it was the time of night — or rather early morning — when one was inclined to be over confidential, and then regret it in the cold light of morning . . .

She was conscious of a sense of shock — a kind of electric communication between them — almost tangible as she felt him stand very close to her now . . .

It was as if he sensed it too for he put his hand on her shoulder . . . 'Loneliness is a terrible thing, Maggie. The worst kind of affliction. And it's more prevalent today than ever it was, be you young or old. When I was a kid we knew everyone in the street where we lived. Families didn't break up and move away like they do now. When your parents were old it was taken for granted you looked after them. Now no one wants to know . . .'

Margaret thought briefly of her own children. It was certain they didn't need her, probably didn't want her either . . . but Teresa did, even if she didn't realise it.

She touched her cheek tenderly where the girl had kissed it . . .

'I'm boring you,' he said, sensing her distraction . . . 'tell me about yourself, lass.'

What was there to tell, she thought. Since she'd married Hugh, in a way her life had fallen into a routine that was fairly ordinary if not dull — uneventful, apart from the everyday worries of bringing up a family. They'd started out with little enough, and he had had to work hard to reach the position he was in now. Maybe that was why they had drifted apart, business commitments had taken up more and more of his time.

Now he was prospering, they had a large and comfortable home, and two kids who couldn't care less . . .

But she didn't want to talk about it to Sam. That life was in a kind of separate, water tight compartment . . .

Now he put out his hand, drawing her to her feet.

'There's something you could do about my loneliness, you know that?'

He cocked an eyebrow at her.

Then with the same suddenness that Teresa had moved, he bent and kissed her on the lips. To his surprise the emotion he felt was an overwhelming compassion for her, he sensed a deep

116

loneliness similar to his own, he could feel the warmth and softness of her shoulders under the flimsy dressing gown, and yet she was shivering. It was a protective kind of compassion as one would feel for a small child shut out in darkness and rain . . .

Her hair was soft and fragrant against his face, and the perfume she used reminded him — improbably — of a summer when, as a boy, he'd gone camping on the Yorkshire moors near his home — of ferns, and moss, and the damp greenness of out of doors . . .

For a moment she leant against him, surrendering herself to the comfort of his arms — then she stiffened and gently disengaged herself . . .

'Good night — and thank you for not going to the police. I'll promise to do all I can to find out who took the money, and to make certain it doesn't happen again . . . '

Sam chuckled to himself as he poured a last nightcap. The cunning lass — he hadn't actually made any

117

such promise — and she knew he knew it!

As Margaret passed Teresa's room on her way to bed, she saw the door was ajar, and put her head round to say good night and reassure her once more. But the girl lay with her eyes closed.

The room was bare and characterless as a prison cell, and not much more cheerful, she thought — no photographs, no books — just a cheap embroidered pyjama case on the chair by the bed, and sitting on it, a battered, moth eaten teddy bear with boot button eyes — probably handed down from one child to another in the Orphanage — how Teresa had managed to keep it she couldn't imagine — maybe the nuns thought it was too far gone to pass on . . .

The sight made her heart ache with love, with longing . . . she thought of all the girl had missed in her childhood — joys and excitement that could never be compensated for — a mother's love, a warm home background, someone to care deeply.

She sighed. There was nothing now she could do about the past, but somehow she was going to ensure the future made up in some small measure for the unhappiness for which she had been responsible . . .

'I'll have the room repapered and painted,' she thought, 'hang one or two nice prints on the wall, try to make it a little bit more home like. Maybe that would help.'

Softly she closed the door . . .

6

As Margaret undressed, thinking about Teresa — the word Home brought a stab of guilt. There were the ties and responsibilities she had left behind to be considered. Things she was neglecting. She rang Muriel twice a week to make sure everything was running smoothly, she also checked on all the local happenings with her — how the garden was looking, if the fruit had been picked and bottled, the usual pounds of jam made, for she had to write a weekly letter to Hugh giving him all the little homely details — and send it to Muriel to post in the village.

How true it was as her mother had so often said 'Oh what a tangled web we weave, when first we practise to deceive!'

She'd certainly involved herself in a complicated situation — but she was more certain as each day passed that in the end it would all be worth while . . .

She lay in bed, thinking now of Hugh and Tim and Linda . . .

Strangely enough, now she'd been away from them all for the first time since her marriage, she had had a change in her attitude — 'a sea change' she thought — it was a feeling of warmth and affection which had been missing lately.

Maybe distance had allowed her to put things into their true perspective.

Now she blamed herself more than she had before for the children's casual attitude. They had been spoilt admittedly, given a free rein. Perhaps in a way it had been a reaction against the misery and deprivation of her own childhood . . . and the feeling of guilt which had increased with the years, about her other child — Teresa . . . It was as if she had to over indulge Tim and Linda to compensate in some way . . . she knew of course that was ridiculous, but the very fact of having now done something concrete had at least lightened her spirit a little.

Oddly enough too, the feelings she had for Sam had in a way heightened the perception of her emotion for Hugh. She missed him badly, the unfailing support his presence always gave her, his wisdom in a crisis. She felt lonely, only half a person without him.

It was true in latter years they had to a certain extent lost the art of communication — when two people had been married for two decades they took a tremendous amount for granted, but there were so many little things they shared, things known only to themselves that were precious, moments that could never be told . . .

And when Tim had been born, Hugh had been so proud. They hadn't had much money to spare in those days, Hugh had been a very small cog in the wheel of the firm where he was now a partner, but he'd given her all the little luxuries he could, brought her red roses out of season, made her feel wanted, precious.

They'd been close then . . .

When Linda came along they'd had a little more money, moved up in the world a bit, that's why they'd been able to ask Muriel to come and live with them.

Maybe it was at that time the subtle change had started in their relationship. Hugh had been aiming high, absorbed in work, stayed later and later at the office — she had felt resentful, neglected even, behaved like a petulant child probably — and yet now as she thought about it she realised it had all been done for her benefit . . .

And then, as she had more time to think, she'd became more and more obsessed over the idea of finding Teresa . . . in a way, although Hugh wasn't even aware of her existence, she had come between them . . .

She wished now with all her heart that she had confided in him years ago when they were first married.

Now, with the passing of the years, it became increasingly difficult. It would be asking a lot to beg for forgiveness now she had lived a lie for so long . . .

On the phone the day before, Muriel had assured her the children were perfectly all right — what she saw of them.

'They've put out one or two feelers about you of course,' she told Margaret, 'tried to wheedle your address out of me but I've fobbed them off by saying you're moving about, visiting friends. I told them if they want any message passed on, I'll let you have it. They seem to think the strangest part is that you didn't take the car . . . they can't imagine anyone having to travel around by British Rail from choice . . . '

'I know,' she replied, 'and I wish I had brought it now, but at the time it seemed the wise thing to do.' She paused, 'I hope to be finished here in about three weeks — if you can keep them at bay.' She smiled to herself at the expression, 'I don't intend to make them sound like a couple of ravening wolves — but you know what I mean.'

'I'll do my best,' the reassuring voice floated over the wire, 'so long as things your end are working out . . .'

'I think I can say they are.' Margaret thought for a moment of Teresa's impulsive kiss, and wished she could tell someone about it. Someone who would really understand. It would have been wonderful to be able to tell Hugh himself. He'd always been a tower of strength in a crisis. When Linda had been thrown from her pony and remained unconscious for so long . . . when Tim had an accident on his motor bike, it was Hugh who sat with him till the doctor came.

Sometimes she felt she'd been pretty useless, utterly dependent on him, and then repaid his love and care by being moody and unapproachable when thoughts of her daughter filled her mind.

Perhaps now, when they were together again, things would have changed, maybe these few weeks would have softened her, increased her understanding so that she could get back on the old footing with Hugh, her mind set at rest.

In the early days their love had been a wonderous, precious thing to her. Hugh had been passionate, yet always gentle and considerate. A perfect lover.

Now she thought of Sam — he was attractive in an earthy kind of way, there was no denying that — but there was some quality in Hugh which Sam could never achieve — something she couldn't put into words . . .

She turned over, watching the reflection of the street lamp on the ceiling — the branches of a tree in the road threw patterns against the dingy paper . . .

In some ways she longed for the weeks to pass, to get home again, but in others she would have liked to slow the time down — she was determined to finish the task she had chosen.

It was several days later when

Margaret had been shopping, she got back to the Pack Horse shortly before dinner and found things strangely silent.

A couple of people sat in the bar chatting to Joe, the dining room door was open and the tables laid up all right, but there was no sign of either Teresa or Sam . . .

For some reason a feeling of foreboding crept over her . . .

She took off her hat and put it on the desk. Then she went through the green baize door into the kitchen. The warm, appetising smell of cooking greeted her. But still no Teresa, and the cook hadn't seen her since lunch . . .

Maybe she's still in her room changing, Margaret thought, although it was really time she was on duty in case some early diners came in . . . she glanced at her watch, then checked the various dishes to be served for dinner, and turned to go back again into reception. As she did so, Teresa came rushing down the stairs, almost tripping in her haste.

'What on earth's the matter?' Margaret asked.

'Oh Mrs Smith, thank goodness you've come. I've been up to your room to look for you, I didn't realise you were out. It's Tad . . . I've tried to see him but he's gone, disappeared . . . '

Margaret took her arm and led her into the office.

'Now sit down and tell me exactly what happened — where can't you find him and why were you looking for him?' As she spoke she rang the bell for some coffee.

'We arranged to go out for a little while this afternoon while I was off duty, and have a cup or tea at the café. I went there and waited and waited, and then just as I was leaving to come back here, the fellow Tad lives with in the caravan came up to me — he recognised me from a photo Tad had of me — I'd never seen him before . . . ' she gulped, half crying.

'Take it slowly,' Margaret said gently.

'Well it seems he went to Plymouth, like I told you he was going to, and he's got a job there — but that's not what I'm worried about — even if it means I won't see so much of him,' she was sobbing now and had to stop talking for a moment.

Margaret put her arm round her. 'Here love, drink this, it's hot and sweet.' She waited while the girl swallowed some of the coffee.

'Then his friend told me he'd admitted taking some money from the cash box in the dining room here — I think in a way he was quite pleased to think he'd been so clever, taking it right under our noses without being found out. Apparently he needed it to buy some decent clothes for the interview ... I don't know if he guessed his friend would tell me so I'd be able to tell Mr Perrett I hadn't taken it ... '

Margaret thought privately it was highly unlikely, from what she'd seen of Tad, his attitude had been typically 'I'm all right Jack ... ' but she waited for Teresa to go on.

'If that was it, then I'm glad, and at least he'll have to believe me that I didn't take it now — Mr Perrett I mean,' her voice held a faint note of defiance ... 'but I must say it was still a bit of a shock — in spite of what you and I had talked about the other night — him taking the money — I didn't think he was a thief — not so as to get me into trouble ... '

'Don't think about it too much, life is full of these kind of surprises I'm afraid, we just have to learn to live with them. And none of us can say how we'd react in different circumstances, if we're very tempted ... but it was a bit stupid of him to steal, specially in a small town like this. He was bound to be found out in the end ... ' She remembered how his eyes had fastened on her diamond ring ...

Teresa nodded. 'I know. I wish now I'd done something more for him, or asked if he was short of cash. At least I could have lent him some till he got settled . . . '

'We're all a bit inclined to say 'if only' after the event,' Margaret said . . .

'Well, as I said before, not everyone's as kind as you are, but I think the trouble with Tad is, the more money you give him, the more he's going to want. I was beginning to realise that . . . '

And not only people like Tad, Margaret thought, her mind on Linda and Tim who both seemed to have bottomless pockets when it came to money, and thought their father had too . . .

'He wasn't a bad artist though,' Teresa went on slowly, 'when he wasn't trying to be 'with it . . . ' Trouble was materials were so expensive . . . he gave me a couple of his pictures. I'd like to show them to you . . . '

The tears had stopped now.

'I'd love to see them, and I tell you what, I'm going to get your bedroom done up, papered and painted. We'll choose the colours together, and maybe we can find you a bookcase and some books, then you could have the pictures framed and hang them up, couldn't you?'

The girl looked a little doubtful for a moment. 'I'd like the room done up, and thank you very much, but I'm not sure about the paintings . . . '

She stood up, composed now . . . 'I must look the most frightful sight, but I felt so upset with him going away, and the money and everything.'

Margaret patted her hand. 'You go and wash your face and I'll take over in the dining room till you're ready . . . O.K.?'

'Thank you Mrs Smith, you're quite the kindest person I've ever met.' Once again she gave Margaret a quick soft kiss on the cheek and was gone.

Margaret smiled to herself. At least it was a healthy sign that Teresa had started to care how she looked . . .

She told Sam about Tad directly he

got back from Exeter, where he'd been on business.

'I'm glad. As much for your sake as anyone's, lass. It wasn't very pleasant to have that kind of thing hanging over us. And at least maybe it'll keep him away from your girl. Perhaps she'll find herself a nice young man now you've improved her looks and brought her out a bit. There's plenty about these parts I reckon, young farmers and such . . . why don't you give her a little encouragement in the right direction eh?' He smiled at Margaret, putting a finger down one side of his nose and winking in a conspiratorial manner . . .

'I've no intention of interfering or trying to be a matchmaker,' she said quickly, 'she must choose her own friends, live her own life, learn to discriminate like we all have to . . . '

Sam smiled. 'Then as a mother you'll be quite unique, most of them can't keep their fingers from meddling where daughters are concerned.'

'She's twenty one, and after all she's

looked after herself till now,' Margaret said, 'there are some things best left alone . . . '

But it hadn't escaped her notice that on Market Day there was one particular young man who made a point of having his lunch at the Pack Horse, and she'd seen his eyes following Teresa round the room with admiration . . . the girl had of course been too wrapped up in Tad to notice . . .

The young man was usually with an older woman who Margaret imagined was his mother, and she guessed he brought her in to do her shopping on Wednesdays. She made a few discreet enquiries from Joe, who knew everyone — and their business — in that part of Devon, and he confirmed what she had thought.

'That's young Andy Rossiter. His father's one of the biggest farmers in these parts. Breeds South Devons, always stuck to them, and they're coming back into fashion now, selling abroad even I hear. He's go ahead all right, and young Andy's the apple of his eye, an only one, be a rich young man one day . . . ' he paused, 'he's not engaged either, since he left Agricultural College all his time's taken up helping his Dad, and he's keen on engineering too, designed one or two useful bits of machinery 'tis said . . . nice young chap, Andy, any girl'd be lucky to have him for husband . . . '

Margaret decided to keep her fingers crossed and to try to refrain from pushing her luck — or rather Teresa's, and it was as if the gods had indeed played into her hands, for a few days later she saw Andy waiting by the reception desk as she came down the stairs. She smiled at him, 'Can I help you?'

He shifted a little uneasily from one foot to the other, then he said, 'My mother was really going to talk to you about it, but she's in bed with a bad cold so she couldn't come in with me today . . . '

'Oh, I am sorry, it's the changeable

weather I expect, there are lots of colds about, I do hope she'll soon be better. Meanwhile what can I do for you,' Margaret said.

'It's like this. We're having a Barn Dance the week after next, we have one each year actually, and usually Mum and one or two of our neighbours do the catering, but we thought this year we'd like to get someone from outside, professionals as you might say — it's got a bit out of hand with all the visitors in the area who like to come along. And the food's so good in the dining room here lately, we wondered if you ever did things like that . . . '

Margaret hesitated only for a moment. This was too good an opportunity to turn down, but she knew that soon she would have to make up her mind to return home, and Sam had never done any outside catering. But she had had plenty of experience with organising church fetes, garden parties and so on — a Barn Dance would be a cinch . . . not only that, she could send Teresa over to the farm to help . . .

Thinking her long silence must mean the answer was in the negative, Andy said 'I was afraid you might think it a bit too much to ask . . . '

'Oh I don't, it isn't that at all,' she said quickly, 'quite the contrary in fact. I was just working out one or two things in my mind. But I think it would be very good for business if we did branch out a little. Could you give me until tomorrow to decide? I'll have to discuss it with Mr Perrett of course — and perhaps you could give me some idea of numbers so we can get down to the cost, menus etc . . . how would that be?'

He smiled widely. 'Just super. Mum will be thrilled . . . '

He paused a moment and looked round to see if anyone was listening, then he leant nearer Margaret and said confidentially, 'I suppose . . . I mean would there be any chance of letting us have a waitress, just to serve at the buffet? We usually have a long table with food on, and another for the bar, there's always plenty of volunteers for the drinks section, but not so many for the food! Of course we'd pay whatever the charge you felt necessary,' he added quickly.

Margaret could hardly believe her luck and the fact that they both had similar ideas about Teresa! She was willing to bet it hadn't been his mother's suggestion to include a waitress in the arrangements!'

'I'm sure we could fix that. I don't suppose you'd need her till the dinners here are finished, and anyway I could relieve her myself if necessary in the dining room.'

'Oh thanks, I'll pop back tomorrow and see what you've decided . . . '

He ran down the steps to his Land Rover with a cheery wave of his hand. Margaret watched him — yes, he was just the sort of boy she would like for Teresa . . .

Sam wasn't keen on the idea at first.

'Lot of work, carting all the china and so on over, be breakages too when they get some of that rough cider inside them, all those young folk . . . '

'Don't be stuffy,' Margaret said. 'If you go into it properly you'll make a nice little profit, and they have to pay for anything they break anyway.'

He smiled in spite of himself. 'Oh all right, I can see you've set your mind on it, if you like to do all the work, carry on. Trouble with you is, lass, you'd charm the birds down off the trees, poor old Sam hasn't a chance.'

Later that evening Margaret told Teresa about the idea of her going to the farm to help with the Barn Dance. Much to her relief, the girl's face lit up with pleasure. 'I'd love it, I've never really been on a farm. And I love the country. Do you think I'd have a chance to look at the animals?'

'I don't know if there'd be much time for that on this particular occasion, but maybe Andy would take you round some other time, show you the whole farm . . . '

Teresa's face fell. 'I'd rather go on my own, round the farm I mean. I've finished with men,' she said vehemently. 'I just don't trust them any more after that Tad.'

'They're not all the same you know,' Margaret said gently, 'you mustn't condemn the whole sex just because of one member of it . . . '

The girl looked at her and suddenly some of the old sullen look had returned to her eyes.

'It isn't just one member of it — I guess I pick them badly, even my father must have been rotten, leaving my mother with a baby and not marrying her . . . '

For a moment Margaret felt quite dizzy, she gripped the side of the desk, her eyes closed. When she opened them again, the girl had gone, slamming the door behind her . . .

7

Margaret sat down quickly in the nearest chair before her legs should crumple beneath her, covering her face with her hands. Teresa's words as she left the room still echoed in her ears —

'Even my father must have been rotten — leaving my mother with a baby and not marrying her . . . '

Obviously the girl hadn't the slightest idea how the words had hurt her when she'd said she felt there was some inherent weakness in herself that made her pick the wrong men — like Tad — but it was almost as if she did know . . .

Sam had seen the whole incident from the other side of the hall, and when Teresa came out of the office, banging the door behind her, he crossed quickly and went in to Margaret . . .

'What's wrong lass — what was all that about, eh?'

She looked up at him, her face drawn, her eyes full of pain . . .

'You look as if you've seen a ghost, Maggie love . . . '

'In a way I have I suppose — the ghost of myself at seventeen when I too thought all men were rotten — like Mike, Teresa's father . . . '

She repeated what the girl had just said, her voice breaking as she finished the telling . . .

He rested his hand gently on her shoulder.

'Don't take it too much to heart, she's upset at the moment over the boy, understandably — none of us like to think we're bad judges of character, that we've been conned where our friends are concerned. And you must remember she's very immature for her age, more like a teenager than a woman of twenty one — which she is.' He paused, 'she's going through a difficult time, Maggie love . . . '

He was about to add — specially under her circumstances — but thought better of rubbing salt in the open wound which he knew existed in Margaret's heart.

For a moment she leaned her cheek on his hand.

'You have a wonderful knack of cheering me up, putting things into their true perspective. I imagine that stems from that good Yorkshire common sense.' She gave him a weak smile. 'And while we're on the subject of Teresa, I've been meaning to ask you — I'd like to have her room done up, redecorated. Nothing elaborate, and I'll pay half . . .'

She felt the sudden, urgent need to do something tangible for the girl, to compensate, to shake her from the grey depths into which she seemed to have sunk.

Sam sighed. 'Have it done by all means, and yours as well.'

He took a cigarette from the box on the desk and lit it, flinging the match into the wastepaper basket with an impatient flick of his wrist as he said with some heat, 'I hate you sleeping up there, it isn't as if it's necessary. We don't depend entirely on residents like a boarding house, for our profits. And one small room wouldn't make all that much difference,' his voice was pleading.

Margaret had to smile. She knew well enough what was in the back of his mind as he made the suggestion.

'Look — I'm sorry but doing up my room, or changing it for a better one even, isn't going to persuade me into staying beyond the time I promised. But I will arrange to have them both done — and thank you. It shouldn't take more than a couple of days, so it won't mean either of us taking up a resident's bedroom for more than one night probably . . . '

Sam shrugged his shoulders. 'I might just as well talk to myself I suppose, you'll do what you want anyway, you're a very determined, self-sufficient woman, Maggie . . . ' but he grinned to take the sting from the words . . .

She got up and stood looking at him for a moment, then she said quietly, 'Determined I may be, but self-sufficient no Sam, underneath I'm just as vulnerable and uncertain as the rest of the human race.' She dropped a kiss on his cheek as she went from the room, and felt his eyes watching her . . . Sam was becoming quite a problem and one she wasn't sure how she was going to solve.

But now she wasted no time. She rang up a local builder by the name of Brooking, one of Joe the barman's pals, and he arrived the same afternoon armed with enormous books of wall-paper patterns and cards of shiny paint samples.

She went to look for Teresa, and found her polishing the cutlery in the dining room. It was surprising what an interest she took now in her job, keeping fresh flowers on the tables, making sure the mats were clean and the dark wood well polished . . .

'Come and have a look at these colours for the two bedrooms. I'd like you to help me choose the most suitable,' she said. Teresa smiled at her and Margaret felt a sense of relief that she seemed to have got over the Tad episode for the moment anyway . . .

Margaret watched her as she turned the pages of samples, her face had become absorbed, totally interested . . .

'I like this one with the bunches of roses,' she said at last, 'you feel as if you can almost smell them.' She looked up at Mr Brooking and then smiled at Margaret. 'Mind you I expect I'm being terribly square and not 'with it', but that's the kind of wallpaper I like . . . '

The man nodded. 'Actually it's a very good choice Miss, for the rooms you have in mind, it'll wear well too with that all over pattern.' He unfolded the paint card, 'Now how about having the woodwork done this pale honey shade? It matches up fine with the petals of that rose which is repeated so often in the pattern, and it'd give a warm lift to the rooms, they face north if I remember rightly.'

'They do,' Margaret said, 'and pretty grim they are with those tiny windows, but it's surprising what new paper and a lick of paint will do, and we'll see if we can stretch the budget to some new curtains as well, repeating the rose theme I think . . . How soon could you do them?'

He stroked his chin. 'Well, we're kind of between seasons at the moment, people have finished the burst of spring cleaning and decorating, and the October gales aren't lifting the roof tiles yet, so I could do them at the end of the week, if that suits. Work Sunday too, and be finished Monday. The shelves you asked for an' all I reckon.'

Margaret beamed at him. 'How delightful to meet someone who doesn't want to put everything off for at least a month. That's fine, we'll get the rooms cleared for you.'

She'd already found an old sewing

machine in the linen room. 'See if you can find an oil can Teresa, I know this looks a bit as if Queen Victoria herself must have used it, but I had one like it once, years ago, and I think we can soon put it in running order to make the curtains . . . '

Together they measured the windows and chose some rose scattered material at the drapers.

Teresa had entered whole-heartedly into the alterations and decorations, Margaret had never seen her so animated, and she was surprisingly deft and neat with her fingers, taking over the actual making of the curtains once Margaret had showed her how.

She felt guilty as she watched her that she'd never given Linda more encouragement in such ordinary tasks — always she'd taken it for granted it was better to do them herself, or get Muriel to deal with them.

But perhaps if she had asked her daughter she too would have enjoyed helping, like Teresa was now — she had no one but herself to blame that she had never given her the chance . . .

'Have you ever made any of your own clothes?' she asked, as she took the finished curtains from her and pushed the hooks through the tape.

Teresa shook her head. 'No, we only did plain sewing and mending at the Orphanage. Usually on awful thick material that made your fingers sore, and mostly just nighties and pyjamas for the little ones. You couldn't make them look pretty, and somehow I've never had the nerve — or the cash — to buy a pattern and try myself in case I made a hash of it and wasted the material. It's different if you've got someone to show you, help you — and it's more fun with two anyway . . . '

Margaret looked away, remembering Linda's half-hearted attempt with expensive patterns and yards of flowered silk, usually she got bored half-way through and Muriel had been pressed into finishing the dress, or whatever, which she also usually ended up

149

wearing as Linda scorned what she called 'draggy home made stuff . . . '

'We'll go to the shop after lunch and get a length of material to make you a dress for the barn dance evening, and some cotton as well for day dresses. If we get a simple pattern, you'll see just how easy it is. And it's always nice to know no one else will have anything quite the same.'

Teresa beamed at her. 'Would you really? That would be super . . . '

How easily the girl was pleased, Margaret thought.

As soon as the two rooms were done, Margaret carried the sewing machine into Teresa's room. It smelt fresh and clean of paint. Together they hung the new curtains and stood back to admire the result.

'You'd never believe you could transform something so easily would you?' Teresa said softly, looking round.

Without answering, Margaret unwrapped the jade green silk which Teresa had chosen for her new dress. They cut it and fitted it and holding the tacked pieces up against her Margaret thought how beautifully the colour suited her, bringing out the lights in her eyes, contrasting with the colour of her hair . . .

Her eyes were shining with excitement, her lips parted in a half smile. What a pretty mouth she has when she smiles, and beautiful even teeth . . . Margaret thought, remembering with a shock that she could have been looking at Mike — Mike whom she thought she had forgotten, locked away in the past . . . living again in his daughter . . .

'I just can't believe it,' Teresa said slowly, 'all this, just for me. It's like having a little home of my own, as if I really do belong somewhere at last,' she sighed, 'I'll never want to leave . . . '

'Oh you will, one day, when you get married and have a real place of your own,' Margaret said, biting through a thread of cotton as she finished off the hem on the green dress.

Teresa got to her feet. 'I almost

forgot, I promised to show you Tad's paintings didn't I?'

She went over to the cupboard and brought out two canvasses. She held up the first. It showed a young chestnut foal, gambolling in a meadow of golden buttercups, and although the composition was not perfect, it somehow had captured and conveyed a feeling of warm sunshine, of colour and movement.

'I like that very much,' Margaret said.

'It's called High Noon.' She put it down and picked up the other, giving a little giggle as she held it up in front of Margaret. 'You'll never guess what this one's called — or what it's meant to be . . .'

It was a wild daub of bright colours, laid on thick, probably with a palette knife — whirls and streaks, patches and zig zags like something out of a nightmare — it almost gave Margaret a headache just to look at it . . .

'I must admit I like the first one best.

But I expect that's because I'm too square to appreciate modern art,' she smiled.

Teresa grinned back like a fellow conspirator. 'I agree. As a matter of fact I told Tad so, and he said it was typical of the kind of bourgeois person I am and that I could only appreciate the obvious, the blatant. That this one is perfectly descriptive of the artist's idea and would immediately be recognised by another artist . . . I can remember his exact words. They hurt me at the time . . . '

'Well what is it called?' Margaret asked, wondering how on earth anything so formless could represent anything tangible. It could equally well have been looked at upside down without making any appreciable difference as far as she could see . . .

Teresa read from the back of the canvas, 'It's called HELL'S KITCHEN.'

She looked at Margaret and suddenly they both started to laugh, until the tears ran down their cheeks.

'It couldn't possibly be called anything else could it?' Teresa gulped at last, when she could manage to get the words out.

Margaret supposed it wasn't really all that funny, but it had struck a chord somewhere, released even more the tension between the two of them and swept away the last remaining barrier that had existed, put them somehow on an equal footing so there was a point of real contact at last . . .

She wiped her eyes, and bent to kiss the girl's soft cheek as she picked up her sewing once more.

She knew now there would be no rebuff to her advance — it was as any mother might kiss her daughter. The sound of the girl's spontaneous laughter brought an involuntary smile to her lips hours later as she remembered it.

She'd never heard her laugh before and it seemed the most marvellous sound she could imagine . . .

The next morning she sat checking the bookings in the office. 'You ought to go up and look at those two rooms,' she said to Sam, who was watching her from the other side of the desk. 'You'd never believe what a difference it's made, and that man's charges are most reasonable. I think you ought to make an effort to have some of the other rooms done too . . . '

He nodded. 'Yes love, I daresay I'll get around to it . . . but meantime how about you taking an hour or two off? You haven't had any time off at all since you've been here. There's two days racing at Bushel, as you probably realise from the bookings, and the returns in the dining room and bar, so how about coming with old Sam to watch the nags going over the sticks — eh?'

She looked dubious, 'I don't think we ought both to be missing, someone ought to be on duty . . . '

'Why?' he said with true north country brashness, 'We haven't any rooms to let as you can see, we're full right up, so if anyone does come we can't take 'em in. We'll be back before dinner's due to be served . . . ' He hesitated and then grinned at her like a cheeky schoolboy, 'I know, how about showing young Teresa how much faith we've got in her by leaving her in charge? I know you think the sun shines out of her any road,' he added wickedly, the smile on his lips softening the words . . .

'I suppose I could ask Joe to stay on when the bar closes at lunch time, he could have his meal in the dining room instead of going home . . . he and Teresa get on well enough, and between them they could probably cope with any emergency which might arise . . . ' she said slowly.

He threw back his head and roared with laughter at the serious expression on her face. 'If the pub catches fire they can only send for the Fire Engine, same as you and me would, and splash about with the extinguishers to keep the Insurance people happy . . . That's settled then.' He rubbed his hands with pleasure at having got his own way. 'It'll be good for the little lass to take control, know we trust her. She's improved lately, I'll say that for her, or perhaps you . . . '

Margaret had to smile, this was praise indeed from the usually taciturn Sam.

'I think she's weathered the Tad crisis, and doing up her room has given her a moral boost. As I said, you must go up and look at those rooms — we're very ritzy up on the top floor now, better by far than the residents' rooms . . . '

He was just going to say 'Does that mean you'll stay on a bit longer?' When as if she'd read his mind, she said quickly . . .

'You'll find it much easier to persuade someone to take on my job if their quarters are comfortable, it stands to reason.'

Just then the phone rang insistently, drowning whatever reply he had been about to make . . .

★ ★ ★

Margaret had never been to a race meeting before, and by the time they managed to get through the heavy traffic, the second race had started, but the sun, and clear fresh air, the smell of newly mown grass, made her feel quite light hearted.

They stood on a little rise overlooking the course — she'd said it was a waste of money to go into the paddock when they could drive the car right to the edge of the track — the scene spread out before her was beautiful with the sleek, graceful movements of the horses, the colourful silks of the riders fluttering in the breeze. The lines of shining cars, the masses of people, and in the far distance, the line of the moor, a purple haze in the summer heat.

She glanced at Sam standing beside her, and felt a little thrill at his nearness. He looked quite handsome in a rugged way in his white polo-necked sweater and brown slacks, his glasses slung round his neck on a leather thong.

On a sudden impulse she slipped her arm through his, and he glanced down at her, his expression a mixture of surprise and pleasure . . .

'Hey, what's that in aid of?'

She couldn't explain it was because of a lessening of tension inside her for a little while, a sudden uprush of joy as she felt at last she had made a breakthrough with Teresa and was starting to repay the debt she owed — for a moment at least all was right in both her worlds . . .

'Just that it's nice to have a day out with the boss,' she said lightly, by way of explanation.

He squeezed her arm to his side. 'Well stop looking at me like that or I shall kiss you in front of all these thousands of people,' he laughed down at her.

'Pick me a winner instead,' she said swiftly before he should make the idea reality . . .

He led her to the enclosure and she held tightly to his arm, quite confused by the milling crowds, listening to the patter of the bookies, watching the tic tac men, some in white gloves waving their arms in wild signals to the inner ring, some with short wave radios . . .

The fresh air had brought colour to her cheeks as she forgot for a moment the problems and complications that surrounded her . . .

What is more the horse Sam picked romped home at five to one . . .

They had places too in the next couple of races, and it looked as if the one they had backed in the last race at twenty to one was a cert . . . Sam was like a small child. He shouted the horse's name and banged his fist on the rails as the horses thundered past, turf flying up from their hooves. Margaret found herself laughing and chattering too as they rushed to be first in the queue at the pay-out window of the tote where she had put her money, having a kind of natural distrust of the bookies . . . their number had gone in first in the frame . . .

Sam hugged her to him. 'We'll celebrate with champers and a nice big bottle of your favourite perfume . . . '

She was astonished at the bundle of notes he pressed into her hand.

'I can't have won all this. However much did you have to put on?'

'Two pounds, all our other winnings, but don't get gambling fever lass, one swallow doesn't make a summer!'

Back in the car she counted out five crisp new notes and gave them back to him. 'That's what I owe for the missing dinner money Tad took.'

He looked at her in complete bewilderment. 'Don't be an idiot, I'll get it back from the Insurance . . . '

She shook her head, 'No, I said I'd pay it back and I want to. I can be just as pig headed as you! And in a way it's a kind of gratitude that Teresa is out of Tad's clutches — which it seems she is — though I wouldn't have wished it to happen exactly as it did I must admit

. . . still, I suppose there's some good in the boy somewhere. He had a pretty rotten childhood I gather . . . '

Sam had to laugh. 'Oh very well.' He folded the notes and put them into his wallet, then he brushed her hair with his lips . . .

She drew back quickly, 'It's late, Sam. I promised Teresa I'd be back in plenty of time before dinner started.'

It was the first time he remembered her using his christian name — maybe it was a good sign, he thought as he started the engine . . .

'O.K. but it's a pity, we could have had a good night out . . . '

'You've got a business to run — and one that could be very successful — and profitable,' she said primly.

He put his hand on her knee. 'I know lass, you're quite right, but I'd like it better if you'd do what I ask — come in as a partner — both business and otherwise, then I could employ staff to do the donkey work. We could have a good life together Maggie, and I know you're not happy in that other life of yours which you carefully keep me away from. What do you say?'

Her immediate reaction was to feel appalled that she'd let Sam think there could be anything in their relationship of a lasting nature, of having allowed him to read more into her feelings than she had intended.

She turned her head away and gazed through the window at the hurrying, laughing, jostling crowd.

She had to admit she hadn't enjoyed herself so much, or felt so carefree and young for years. But was it all due to Sam's company . . . wasn't it partly that the guilt, the cloud of responsibility she had carried for more than twenty years about Teresa, had lifted a little so she could feel free at last to enjoy herself?

But now she owed some kind of debt to Linda and Tim, and Hugh above all, for the times she had rebuffed them, been preoccupied, her loyalties always divided.

She turned back and looked at Sam,

her hand resting briefly on his. 'Thank you, I'm both grateful and honoured by what you ask, but I'm afraid the answer has to be no . . . I wouldn't like to think I've led you to think otherwise . . . '

His face fell like a child who has had its sweets taken from it, but he murmured, 'Well, I suppose you know best — but I thought . . . '

He relapsed into silence, getting out from the race course in the mêlée of traffic took all his concentration, and when they reached the open road that led back to Queensbridge, they were both silent, occupied with their own thoughts . . .

There was a police car standing outside the Pack Horse as Sam drew the car into the kerb . . .

'What the hell do the fuzz want for goodness sake?' he said shortly with a burst of anger — he goes off like a machine gun, Margaret thought . . . 'Hope Joe hasn't been selling drinks after time,' he went on more quietly. 'Heigh ho, there's always something in this business . . . if it isn't one thing 'tis t'ree as they say in Devon. Come on lass, we'd better go and face the music, after the Lord Mayor's show comes the dust cart . . . '

Margaret got out of the car and followed him with a heavy heart. A sense of guilt rose within her — she'd had the feeling they shouldn't both have gone out — anything might have happened — her first fears were for Teresa — and as if in answer to her unspoken thoughts, the girl met them at the door. She was pale as death and had been crying. A police sergeant stood in the hallway, his helmet under one arm, an open notebook in his hand.

'It's Tad . . . '

For a moment Margaret felt as if an old film were being re-run — surely they'd been through all this only a few days ago . . . was history repeating itself . . . and just when the girl seemed to be getting over the affair . . .

'He's dead!'

The words fell like stones into the silence.

For a moment no one moved as if they'd all been turned to statues . . . then the sergeant came forward.

'I'm sorry to have brought bad news Mr Perrett, specially when neither you nor the manageress were here.'

Am I being over sensitive, or is there a note of criticism in his tone, Margaret wondered . . .

'But I can't trace the young man as having any relatives, any next of kin, and as he had this young lady's name and address on a piece of paper in his pocket I had no alternative . . . '

Margaret immediately took charge of the situation, drawing Teresa into the curve of her arm.

'Shall we go into the office? We don't want the guests to be upset . . . '

Teresa had started to sob quietly, hopelessly, murmuring, 'It's all my fault, if I'd been nicer to him, tried more to help, he wouldn't have gone off like he did . . . '

Margaret gave her a little shake. 'Don't talk like that, don't even think like it, whatever you did or didn't do would never have changed his nature, there are many things that people do . . . ' she paused, she was going to say, 'that we cannot hold ourselves responsible for' but she felt Sam's eyes on her. She was confused — not knowing what had caused the boy's death, whether he had been killed in an accident, or taken an overdose — secretly the latter wouldn't have surprised her, he seemed unstable . . .

The sergeant was writing in his notebook, he looked up and said, 'The facts are these — the young man had been taken in for questioning, about some complaints from an art gallery — artists' materials were missing, he was seen to take them . . . but getting out of the police car he managed to escape, then he stole a car, one of our patrols gave chase — unfortunately he lost control of the car and went over the embankment by the new roundabout just on the edge of the city . . . he was dead by the time the ambulance arrived. It must have been instantaneous, there was nothing anyone could have done . . . '

Teresa burst into renewed sobs, burying her head on Margaret's shoulder.

The policeman shifted his weight, he was still young enough, although a sergeant — and human enough to hate this kind of job. He never knew what to say, the trouble was the questions had to be asked . . . he looked at Margaret for comfort . . .

'There are just a couple of questions I have to ask the young lady — it's about some missing money — and the last time she saw Mr Sampson . . . '

For a moment Margaret had lost the thread of the conversation, she hadn't known even that Tad's other name was Sampson . . .

She led Teresa to a chair and handed her a tissue from her bag. 'Look Tess,' the nickname slipped out unconsciously, 'it'll only take a moment to tell the Sergeant what he wants to know, then I suggest you go upstairs and lie down, I'll bring you some tea and a couple of aspirin — a sleep will do you good . . . ' she waved the girl's protestations aside. 'I'll make other arrangements about the dining room tonight, just don't worry . . . '

Teresa managed to answer the policeman's questions in a low voice . . . No, she had no idea who his next of kin would be, he'd been an orphan! The only thing she could suggest was asking the boy who'd shared the caravan with him, he had some kind of scrap metal business she thought . . . but where she had no idea . . .

A large envelope lay on the desk. The policeman pointed to it . . . 'This is his watch, and one or two personal things . . . I wondered if the young lady . . . '

Teresa gulped and shook her head vehemently . . .

'No, please, I'd rather not!'

Once more he glanced appealingly at Margaret.

She stretched out her hand. 'I'll put them in the hotel safe for the time being, perhaps when you've completed your enquiries you can make some arrangements . . . '

The man picked up his helmet, looking relieved as he tucked his notebook into his pocket.

'Thank you, Madam, Mr Perrett, Miss Brown . . . I'm sorry to have had to ask these things, but it's routine, and we didn't know where else to go . . . '

'You did quite right,' Sam said gruffly, thankful for Margaret's calm, reassuring presence. What a woman to be with in a crisis — and at other times, he thought ruefully . . . He saw the sergeant to the door, and Margaret led Teresa upstairs.

'Get undressed and right into bed, the tea and aspirin will make you sleep, you'll feel better then. I'll bring you up something to eat on a tray later . . . '

Going slowly back downstairs she

decided she'd do the waiting in the dining room herself. It promised to be busy with the races so near, and she really couldn't rely on either of the girls in the kitchen . . . long years of watching other people wait on her should be some help, she thought ruefully . . .

The room was packed and to start with she got confused by the different orders, but she explained the waitress was off sick, and she was new to the job . . . and most of the guests were patient and helpful . . . she even made quite a nice sum in tips, and couldn't help smiling to herself as she wondered what on earth Hugh and Linda and Tim would have thought if they could see their mother in Teresa's cap and apron, carrying the loaded trays of chops and vegetables and ice cream from kitchen to dining room . . .

She was exhausted when the last customer had been served, her feet felt as if they were on fire, but she still managed to smile as she showed Sam her bowl of tips . . . and she had to admit she'd enjoyed the challenge. Maybe she was more fitted by birth to this kind of life than the one she had led for the past few years . . .

She took off the cap and apron and went slowly upstairs. Quietly she opened Teresa's bedroom door. To her great relief the girl was fast asleep, some of the colour had returned to her face, although the pillow was damp with tears.

She stood looking down at her . . . although she was naturally sorry Tad had been killed, it was such a waste of a young life — at least now Teresa could start a fresh page . . . she wanted above all her happiness and security . . .

But the matter was not quite concluded, for the next day the sergeant called again to see Sam. As there seemed to be no one at all they could contact over Tad's death and his effects, he was afraid he'd have to ask Miss Brown to go down to the caravan and sort out his few possessions . . .

Sam sent for Teresa and Margaret was cut to the heart at the strained expression which had returned to her face . . . it seemed so unfair that just because she had been out with him a few times she should have to be drawn into all the harrowing machinations of his death . . .

Sam drove them down to Hope's Bay. It was a tiny fishing village with small sandy beaches, and fishing boats drawn up in the harbour, lobster pots and all the paraphernalia of fishing lay about. There was a smell of tar, and fish and the sea which Margaret sniffed appreciatively . . .

The caravan site where Tad had lived was behind the village pub. There were about half a dozen sleazy caravans in an orchard of rough grass. Two dirty urchins played with a mongrel dog, scrap iron, old cars and bedsteads, piles of tyres, and every type of rubbish imaginable lay about in heaps.

An unshaven man leant on the wheel of an old cart, a cigarette butt hanging from his bottom lip.

He leered at Teresa, and stared with undisguised curiosity and antagonism at Sam and Margaret.

This was going to be worse than she had anticipated for the girl . . .

'Tad Sampson's trailer?' He regarded them quizzically. 'That one there — 'ee doan't live there any more though, got hisself killed on the new roundabout at Plymouth . . . only a question of time, I allus said to the wife, the times he's driven back here at night in his pal's car, thought he was Jackie Stewart or summat I guess, driving like the clappers, and half cut I shouldn't wonder . . . ' He paused for a moment to allow this information to sink in and pushed the greasy cap further back on his head. 'You relatives then? Didn't think 'ee had any.'

'No,' Sam said abruptly, 'and all we want to know is which is his caravan if you'd be so civil as to tell us . . . '

The man looked as if he were about to retaliate with a flood of invective,

Margaret shuddered and drew Teresa closer to her — it was obvious Sam's tone had made his hackles rise — but he shrugged his shoulders and pointed to one of the more dilapidated caravans . . .

Its paint was peeling, one window was boarded up with a piece of plywood, one had a sheet of polythene nailed over it where the glass had come away, a gas cylinder stood outside and a rusty bin half filled with trash whose lid had disappeared, leant drunkenly against one wall . . . the smell was appalling . . .

Taking Teresa's arm Margaret said, 'Let's get it over with as quickly as we can. You'd better wait in the car, Sam, I don't trust the look of these people, they'll probably remove the spare wheel while our backs are turned.'

'Shouldn't be at all surprised,' he replied, 'and not only the spare — choose how . . . sure you'll be O.K. lass? Any trouble, and give me a shout . . .'

175

Margaret could feel Teresa shaking as they knocked on the door. There was no reply. Margaret turned the handle . . . the door swung open on rusty hinges.

The inside of the caravan had to be seen to be believed, it was even worse than the outside. Dirty dishes were piled in the small sink, greasy pans littered the tiny cooker, itself so covered in grease it was a wonder any of the jets would light, Margaret thought. Empty beer cans and crisp packets lay on the two single bunks . . .

Teresa shrank back as she stood on the rotting wooden steps . . . 'I don't think I can . . . '

Margaret turned back and drew her hand through her arm. 'Yes you can love, it won't take a moment. We won't bother with anything but his actual clothes and personal stuff. If any of the fixtures and fittings, such as they are — belonged to him I think we'll leave them for the other lad . . . '

His possessions were pathetically few.

Some dirty stained tee shirts with the names of various American Universities printed on them, two pairs of jeans, socks full of holes, some photographs of various girls, some girlie magazines, empty tubes of paint and clotted brushes . . .

Margaret stood looking into the open drawers . . . 'Honestly I don't know what's the best thing to do . . . what would you like done with all this?'

For a moment the girl looked at her, her expression inscrutable . . . when she spoke her voice was very low . . . 'It makes me so angry,' she said slowly, 'a life — someone's whole life, and all that there is at the end to show is this — those shirts,' she pointed to the tee shirts with their inscriptions . . . 'poor Tad, he told me once he'd like to have gone to University, to have had the chance and I suppose those were the nearest he ever got to realising that dream . . . ' her voice broke on a sob . . .

Margaret took her hand. 'Don't upset

yourself, there was nothing anyone could do and I expect he enjoyed his life in his own way . . . none of us really can know what other people are feeling — not all of it anyway . . . '

'Don't you believe it!' Now the girl broke in with surprising vehemence, 'That's what makes me see red — if people don't want kids they've no right to bring them into the world — like Tad and me. If he'd had proper parents — someone to care — to give him a home and some love, he'd still be alive, don't you see? But he never had a chance, all because some woman had a few minutes of pleasure, of passion, whatever you like to call it, resulting in a baby she didn't want, and just gave away to an orphanage as if it were some old clothes she didn't need — shrugged off her responsibility . . . left it to fend for itself . . . however good these places are, they don't care like someone of your own . . . ' she paused a moment, 'it's always been the same for me, that's how I know, that's what we had in common — that no one cared. You wouldn't understand — but if ever I met my mother I'd tell her a few home truths, make her see what she'd done . . . why should they get off like that with no responsibility, no care for what they did?'

Her face now was flushed and her eyes bright . . . Margaret was so taken aback by her outburst that she felt quite dizzy . . . she put out her hand to steady herself against the wall of the caravan . . . but Teresa didn't notice. She'd turned away and was picking over the pathetic clothes . . .

Margaret swallowed, conscious now with complete clarity that any thought she might have had of ever being able to tell Teresa who she was had vanished . . . the small advance she had managed to make was something precious she must cling to — that was for sure . . . but as a friend, a stranger — if she found out then all that would be destroyed, rendered useless.

She sank down on the low bunk, her

legs too weak to stand any longer . . .

Now Teresa turned, her face tear-stained but her eyes dry . . . 'I think we'll leave all this with a note for his friend — his name's Graham. Maybe he can use them. If not he probably knows someone who can. I don't think I can bear to have any of this to remind me . . . I feel so awful about the whole thing.'

She hesitated a moment, then she went on, 'I still feel I should have done more . . . but someone the other day said that when a small child has had no love given to it when it's young — then when it grows up it finds it almost impossible to give love to others . . . I think that could be true . . . it seems to be with me anyway . . . '

Margaret got up slowly — she couldn't trust herself to speak . . . she stepped down from the caravan into the suffocating heat of the afternoon . . . dark clouds massed on the horizon, thunder rumbled in the distance, huge drops of rain spattered on the leaves of the gnarled apple trees, and with relief she hurried to the car where Sam waited with growing impatience as a crowd of dirty urchins had appeared as if by magic, standing in a small circle, staring at him with unwinking gaze . . . he got out quickly as he saw the two women, and opened the doors.

'Thank heaven you've come,' he looked round for Teresa, who was following slowly, 'aren't you bringing anything with you?' he asked, seeing her empty hands . . .

Margaret shook her head quickly — he glanced at her and saw the pain and distress on her face. 'What's the matter Maggie love? Has the girl said something to upset you again?' his voice held a note of impatience . . .

She wondered how he had guessed. For a man he was surprisingly intuitive . . . she nodded briefly, 'In a way, but she didn't know what she was saying, it's not her fault. I don't want to talk about it now . . . '

They drove home in silence as the

storm gathered fury . . . the lightning flashing and zigzagging around them as the thunder seemed as if it would split the sky open, and torrential rain fell from the clouds, making the gutters and drains overflow with the weight of water . . .

Even running from the car to the door of the Pack Horse they got soaked, and Margaret told Teresa to get her wet clothes off and have a bath . . . she would ring the Sergeant and tell him what they had done . . .

She threw off her own soaking coat and ran her fingers through her damp hair while Sam poured her a stiff brandy. 'I know it's tea time, love, but you need that. Now sit down and tell old Sam all about it.'

She took the glass from him with trembling fingers and slowly, word for word, she repeated what Teresa had said. 'I feel like that Queen who had the word 'Calais' engraved into her heart,' she said slowly, 'I'll never forget one sentence she uttered in that dreadful caravan . . . God knows, for what I did wrong I'm being punished. Whether I can ever make up for it I don't know, but I mean to try, even if it means messing up my own life, and one thing I do know, never never is she to find out who I am or any good I have done will be as nothing. Whatever happens the poor child must keep the little bit of confidence, of self respect I have managed to give her . . . '

Wearily she dropped her head on her arms. Sam stood looking down at her, love and compassion spilling from his eyes, and it was with the greatest difficulty he refrained from drawing her into the circle of his arms and repeating the words, 'Marry me, stay with me and I'll make things right for you, look after you Maggie . . . '

But he knew this wasn't the right moment — in fact he wondered if there would ever be a right moment — and in spite of his native Yorkshire phlegm, he longed to ask her to tell him all about herself — and the husband that he knew for certain existed somewhere . . .

All he could cling to was the hope that one day she would choose to tell him so that he might comfort her . . .

8

Margaret was thankful all her spare time, and Teresa's too — was occupied with preparations for the Barn Dance at the Rossiters. There were glasses and china to be washed, cutlery to be polished, linen to be sorted and the ingredients bought for the different snacks Margaret had decided to provide.

Sam watched all the preparations with increasing gloom . . . 'I only hope you're not going and overdoing it, lass, I'm not made of brass you know — worked out your margin of profit have you — with the girl's time and all . . .'

She grinned at him. 'Just leave it to me — I don't think you'll be disappointed.' She was determined it should be a success, not only because she wanted to please Sam, but because in a way it was to be her swan song, for she had made up her mind it was time she thought about returning home. Granted Tad's death had been a slight setback with Teresa in a way, but on the other hand it had brought her closer to Margaret, and now the latter was gambling on her enjoying serving at the Barn Dance, and keeping her fingers crossed that at least she might strike up some kind of friendship with Andy . . .

During the morning and afternoon of the Dance, Sam and Margaret made several journeys over to the farm delivering the china and cutlery, and then in the late afternoon, the boxes and cartons of food. She had eventually prepared most of the food herself, vol au vents, rolls, open sandwiches, pasties and so on — meat pies and sausage rolls she had left to the cook, who really had excelled herself with the lightest puff pastry and juicy fillings . . .

'You get twice as much work out of that woman as I can though she and I are fellow countrymen, as you might say,' Sam grumbled as he helped Margaret pack the foodstuffs.

She grinned, but made no comment, thinking to herself it wasn't what you said so much as how you asked, how you approached people — and the cook herself could be just as touchy as Sam on occasion.

It was a beautiful hot summer day, the air was filled with country smells and when they arrived they found big trestle tables had been set out at one end of the huge thatched barn, the floor had been swept and covered with french chalk, motes of dust danced in the shafts of sunlight, and the air was heavy with the perfume of corn and summer clover . . . she pointed to the floor-boards. 'Look at the width of those planks Sam.'

'Aye lass, reckon they simply sliced the tree up, they're the width of the original trunk of the oak. Been here hundreds of years I daresay, and probably be here for hundreds more

. . . makes you think, feel small, doesn't it?'

At that moment one of the men who milked the cows came into the barn and told them the 'Missis' was expecting them over at the house for tea.

'I'm terribly grateful for all the work and interest you've put into this, Mrs Smith.' She smiled at Margaret, who was gazing round the enormous kitchen with its deep window seats, its rafters with hooks where muslin shrouded hams and bunches of dried herbs hung. An old sheep dog got up stiffly from the rug in front of the stove and came over slowly, wagging his tail, he lifted his eyes at Margaret and she could see they were milky with coming blindness. She put out her hand and stroked the black, silky head.

'That's Fly, father of Smart and Pup, the present sheep dogs. Rossiter sheep dogs go back almost as far as the family itself, and that's into the mists of time,' she smiled, 'and when they get past work, we give them an honourable retirement in the kitchen . . . '

Margaret thought how delightful it was to find people who still cared about the simple things in life and found a dog's old age important . . . She and Sam sat at the long, scrubbed table with its blue and white ringed cups and saucers, dishes of strawberry jam and thick yellow cream, and a huge home made fruit cake. Mrs Rossiter poured the tea, 'Please help yourselves, we have a proper meal later on, but I do like my afternoon tea . . . ' she paused, 'as I was saying, I am so grateful to you for taking over this task, my neighbours and I used to be able to manage, but the whole thing seems to have snowballed beyond our capabilities! And I'm glad too,' she went on slowly, 'that you can spare that nice girl Teresa, she always seems so pleasant when she serves our lunch, such nice manners, it makes it a pleasure to eat at the Pack Horse!'

Margaret warmed to her at once even more, anyone who could praise Teresa was all right in her books . . .

'I always wish I'd had a daughter, but unfortunately I had a bad time when Andy was born and the doctor said no more babies,' she smiled at Margaret. 'Have you any family Mrs Smith?'

For a moment Margaret had forgotten Teresa was not meant to be her daughter, basking in Mrs Rossiter's praise of her . . . now she looked round quickly, but Sam had got up and was the other end of the kitchen examining the enormous deep freeze cabinet which took up the whole length of one wall. She turned back towards the woman and said softly, so her voice wouldn't reach his ears, 'Yes, I'm lucky, I have a pigeon pair, they're nearly grown up now,' she sighed, 'but somehow I don't think Tim, my son, was ever as interested in his home as your Andy is. But I expect that's my fault, not his . . . ' she added almost to herself.

Mrs Rossiter gave her a curious look — she knew she was the new manageress at the Pack Horse of course, and had heard the usual small town rumours about her and Sam, which she had ignored, but she was curious that a woman who seemed somehow to have the stamp of possessions, of money, about her should be working in such a job, and wondered too where the children she spoke of were, and if there was a husband . . . she was about to ask one or two of these questions, when Andy came into the kitchen, the afternoon milking complete . . . he looked bronzed and handsome with sparkling blue eyes like his mother, his sleeves rolled to the elbow showing muscular arms and Margaret felt a surge of maternal longing that this young man could one day become Teresa's husband . . . but immediately she pushed the idea to the back of her mind, she had no right really to hold such thoughts, they rose unbidden . . .

'Hullo Mrs Smith, Mr Perrett. I wondered if we could go over to the barn for a few secs. together to see all the arrangements, Bill told me he'd been up to call you for tea and the place looks super, a complete transformation, he said,' he laughed, 'I can see Mum's nose is going to be properly put out of joint by the experts . . . '

'I'm sure it won't, not if this tea we've just had is an example of her handiwork,' Margaret said, 'I must have put on pounds in weight with that gorgeous cake and that cream . . . good thing I don't live on a farm . . . '

Sam lingered in the kitchen to discuss the finer points of the deep freeze with Mrs Rossiter, he'd been thinking that now business had improved at the hotel, it was something he would need to buy . . .

Andy and Margaret went out of the kitchen door and crossed the yard. The cows who had just been milked, stood round the trough, horning one another out of the way, drinking deep with their lips, then blowing out their cheeks and lifting their heads to stare at them with water running out of their mouths . . . pails rattled in the dairy and somewhere a calf bleated fretfully — she turned back and looked at the old house with its moss patterned roof, a curtain stirred gently in the breeze of an open window and she could imagine the rooms filled with the dry smell of timber — the languid smell of indoor late summer afternoon . . . a kind of torpor hung over it all — soon, she could imagine, to be broken by the shouting and laughter, the music and clapping of the young people — and she was filled with a moment's nostalgia for a kind of youth and way of life she had never known . . . and wished with all her heart Teresa might have a taste of it . . .

The boy was genuinely delighted with what Margaret had provided. 'You've made a super job of it, I can't tell you how grateful I am. Between you and me, it was getting too much for Mum, she gets tired easily these days, and I had a job to make her give it up, but when she sees this, I think she'll be won over . . . everything'll be fine covered with those polythene sheets and it's cooler in here under that thatch than anywhere else . . .'

As they went back across the yard he said hesitantly, 'Mrs Smith, do you think Teresa could come over one afternoon and have a look round? She always seems rather interested in farming and the countryside when she talks to us on Wednesdays at lunch time. She told me she'd never been to the country before she came here, always lived in cities . . . and it's so nice to find someone these days who's interested in something other than discos and the latest pop star! Someone who isn't another Young Farmer I mean.' He looked at her out of the corner of his eyes, smiling hopefully, wondering what her reaction would be . . .

Once more she thought how delightfully refreshing he was for a young man in his early twenties — she could hardly imagine her own son talking like that about a 'dolly bird' or 'chick' or whatever the in word was for girls these days. Maybe it was because he was an only son and spent a good deal of time with his mother . . .

'Why don't you try asking her? She can only say no, and somehow I can't imagine she will.' She crossed her fingers, remembering Teresa's outburst over men recently. 'In fact I can't imagine anyone refusing the chance of spending an hour or two in such a lovely spot,' and with such a charming young man she added to herself.

★ ★ ★

Sam ran Teresa over to the farm, Margaret had been delighted to see the girl had really taken trouble with her appearance, putting on one of the new checked cotton dresses they had made, brushing her hair till it shone, and putting on some bright lipstick . . . she was hardly recognisable compared with the little drab Margaret had first encountered . . .

She heard her come in a little after midnight and longed to call out but thought better of it. She didn't want the girl to think she was too nosey, too curious . . . but next morning it seemed the whole evening had been a great success, all the food had been finished, there had been no breakages, much to Sam's delight, and a nice profit had been made . . . Teresa was full of all that had happened.

'They were all so nice to me, just as if I was one of them,' she kept saying over and over again . . . 'and Andy brought me home in the Land Rover . . . ' she hesitated, 'he's so nice, not a bit like most men of his age . . . ' Margaret grinned to herself, she had heard words just like that only a few hours before . . . 'As a matter of fact,' Teresa went on, not looking at Margaret now, 'he did ask me if I'd like to go over one afternoon and have a look round the farm — that is if I can have the time off . . . '

'I don't think there'd be much difficulty there,' Margaret said smiling . . .

She felt as nervous as if she herself was a young girl again on her first date, longing to tell Teresa what to wear, what to say, to be able to influence her behaviour by remote control, knowing how easily the girl's rather fine sensibilities could be upset by a wrong word or move . . . but she managed to keep her interest and enthusiasms apparently within the bounds of normal interest, although Sam, watching her, grinned and said, 'Honestly Maggie you're just like an old broody hen that's hatched out a duckling . . . I bet you never fussed with your other chicks like this . . . ' She gave him a swift look, but didn't answer, dropping her eyes back to the column of figures she was adding up . . .

The afternoon was warm and sunny with a heat haze hanging over the town, and she wished that she herself could take the next couple of hours off and wander under the shady trees in the cool green fields, but she forced herself to bring the book keeping up to date, to prepare menus for the coming week, though most of the time her attention was anywhere but on the job in hand. She kept glancing at her watch, counting the minutes till Teresa was due to return, her ears strained for the sound of the Land Rover coming up the hill . . .

At last she heard it, and after a slight pause, Teresa's light footsteps running up the steps, calling goodbye to Andy over her shoulder. She sounded so carefree, so happy . . . Margaret let out a long sigh of relief . . . all had gone well.

With difficulty she restrained herself from running across the hall and gathering the girl into her arms . . . Teresa knocked on the office door . . . her hair was tousled by the breeze, there was a faint tan on her cheeks and a powdering of freckles across her nose . . . she stood, transformed, eyes shining, gazing at Margaret . . . it was obvious the bogey of Tad had been laid, they were over that hurdle . . . she must have changed her mind — all men were not like him or her unknown father . . . although, Margaret thought, little does she know how like him she looks at this moment . . . but she said . . .

'Well, how was the country life?'

'Just fab . . . super . . . I can't remember ever having such a marvellous afternoon . . . '

Her face was full of animation, all the drabness had dropped away like the chrysalis from a butterfly, there was a shimmering kind of aura about her . . .

'Everything was so green and fresh — and the trees — we climbed to what I'm sure must have been quite the highest hill in the whole of Devon and we could see the sea . . . ' she paused a moment, 'it seems odd doesn't it, but I'd never seen it before . . . then we started to run like kids, I don't quite know why, it was crazy really, but we just couldn't help it . . . it must have been something to do with all that sun and fresh air — almost a kind of intoxication . . . though I've never been drunk,' she added quickly, 'and Andy said he'd only been a bit merry on cider, but it was the same kind of feeling of elation — only thing is he said with cider you get a hangover, but this kind of drunkenness doesn't leave any after effects — at least he didn't think so . . . ' Margaret could see that as she described the afternoon, she was re-living it in her imagination . . .

'I simply couldn't believe it was all true — and . . . ' she hesitated, her eyes dropping away from Margaret's for a moment, 'you were right, all men aren't like Tad, and my father — Andy's . . . well I've never met anyone like him . . . I didn't believe there were such people . . . '

Her eyes spilled out love — suddenly discovered — and Margaret could guess the whole world spun dizzily like a windmill . . . there was no need for words — her face was transformed with joy, and her mother could remember how once she too had felt . . . but Andy lived in a different world from Mike . . .

'Then we went and watched the cows being milked. I didn't realise they did it with those machine things. I thought at first it must hurt the poor things, but Andy just laughed and said of course it didn't, they wouldn't give down their milk — I think that was the expression he used — if they weren't perfectly happy . . . then there were the pigs . . . I didn't like the great fat sows much,' she wrinkled her nose, 'although I have to admit they didn't smell too bad, and Andy says that really they're the cleanest of creatures if you'll only let them be. And the babies are absolutely adorable . . . I don't think I'll ever be able to eat pork or bacon again!' She had to stop at last to draw breath.

'And you had some tea?' Margaret said, bringing the conversation down to a more earthy level . . .

She nodded, 'Yes, we had it in the

kitchen with the men and Mrs Rossiter.

'She's such a nice person too. Funnily enough she was telling me she was born in the Midlands like me. She met Andy's father when she was camping down here with her school. Isn't that romantic?'

She looked at Margaret with shining eyes. Then she looked away and added, 'She . . . she said she thinks it's a good thing for farmers to marry girls from the town, it keeps a nice even balance.' A faint flush tinged her cheeks. She wasn't sure now if she'd said too much, given away the secret she was hugging in her heart, but she lifted her eyes to Margaret and read there smiling encouragement.

'It's marvellous to feel that someone — well some people can like me just for what I am . . . I'd like my mother to know that in spite of her I am loved . . . '

Once more Margaret felt a stab like a knife wound in her heart. She closed her eyes for a moment, the agony was almost physical . . . but Teresa hadn't noticed as she chattered on . . .

'Mrs Rossiter asked me to go over again on my next half day. Do you think I could?'

Margaret longed to put her arms round her, to say, 'Darling child, your mother does know that people like you just for what you are, that she is sure soon someone will even love you for just what you are, if he doesn't already . . . ' and to hold her close and talk as a mother does to a daughter when she is in love for the very first time . . .

But she said, 'Of course, in fact next week when things quieten down after the races, I think you might have a whole day off, you've worked so hard, it's the least I can do . . . '

The girl bent and kissed her and then, like a small child, skipped away upstairs to change into her working dress and apron . . .

For a long time Margaret sat quite still, staring into space . . . she kept seeing Teresa's joyous face between her and the books she was working on, and it was nearly midnight when at last Sam came into the office after cashing up in the bar.

'Burning the midnight oil, lass? No need for that. You work too hard. Look what Sam's brought you . . . '

He produced a bottle of champagne from behind his back. 'I told you we'd have some after the races, better late than never. A glass of this'll perk you up. Dr Perrett's sure cure for all ills . . . '

He got two glasses from the cupboard and drew the cork from the bottle with a loud pop. The froth bubbled down the sides of the glasses as he poured the sparkling liquid . . .

Margaret sat on the small sofa that stood in one corner of the office and Sam came over and sat beside her . . .

Suddenly she was very conscious of his nearness, of the sound of his voice, deep and kind . . . he had a warmth she had forgotten existed, and an understanding strange in such a brusque manner . . .

She felt very tired, physically and mentally. She would love to have rested her head on his broad shoulder, abandon herself to the luxury of letting him take all the worries from her, to relax completely . . .

She took a sip of the champagne, the cold bubbles tingled on her tongue, and suddenly she knew she could love this man — that possibly even now her marriage was in jeopardy . . . She admitted at last to herself that she had been fighting against the knowledge, against letting herself think about it, but now there was no doubt in her mind that it could happen . . . in trying to dismiss the feeling, to push it from her, she murmured his name, hardly realising she did so . . .

'What is it, Maggie love?' He took her free hand. She stopped, confused, uncertain, knowing that it could not be, he was not for her, nor she for him . . . she had other loyalties, other commitments, so many people were involved, and it would be fair to none of them. All the ramifications were too intricate to contemplate even . . .

As if he knew only too well what was in her mind, he said softly, his voice hardly above a whisper, 'You know I love you, Maggie . . . '

It was a statement, not a question now. Without waiting for a reply he went on, 'We're not kids, not teenagers in the flurry of our first affair. We're adults, lass, mature, we both know what we want . . . I've already told you I can't bear to see you working so hard, sleeping in that awful little room, new wallpaper or not,' he smiled briefly. 'I'd like better things for you, things I can tell you've been used to.' He paused, then said softly, 'can't you tell old Sam about it, love?'

She shook her head, leaning away from him a little, trying to fight the weakness which seemed to be seeping through her . . . 'I wish with all my heart that I could, but at the moment, the way things are, the way I feel, it's just not possible. It's so difficult to explain why — I hardly know myself. I'm living in two worlds I suppose, and I don't want one to intrude on the other . . . ' she hesitated . . . 'and one of those worlds is becoming increasingly dear to me . . . I like you so much Sam — that sounds weak, a complete understatement for what I truly feel — and yet . . . '

'There's someone else, that's it isn't it?' he finished for her, almost roughly now in his disappointment.

She nodded slowly, hating all the while to hurt him, but knowing she must, certain the half truth would be more painful to a man like him than the whole — that his own brash honesty sought the same from her . . .

'You could say that I suppose, yes . . . '

And yet does Hugh really need me as much as you do, she thought for a moment. Do the kids want me like Teresa does . . . where do I belong . . .

where do my ultimate loyalties lie . . . if here, then was it only because I want to help Teresa, or does it go deeper . . . is it that I can't leave this man I have grown to love as well as respect, for whom I feel such a deep affinity which I never seem to have had with Hugh . . .

The time was rapidly approaching when she would have to make the choice, to weigh in the balance the needs of all those whom she loved, who depended on her, and whom she wanted to help.

Sam got up slowly and poured himself another glass of champagne. Then he came back and sat beside her again. Gently he stroked her hair, murmuring her name as if she were a small child in need of comfort.

'Whatever happens, lass, I'll always be here if you need me, you only have to ask, there's nothing I wouldn't do for you, you know . . . '

She nodded, her head resting now on his shoulder, her body inclined towards him by the angle of the sofa, until at last he realised she had fallen asleep through sheer exhaustion.

Gently he put a cushion behind her head and tucked a rug round her. Then he turned out the overhead light, leaving only the desk lamp, and tiptoed away . . .

* * *

The phone bell burst shrilly into her subconscious . . . she tried to pull herself up from the cloying depths of sleep . . .

For a moment she couldn't think where she was . . . the champagne had left her dizzy, her mouth dry, and the angle she had been lying at had given her a crick in the neck . . .

She sat up, rubbing at her eyes, glancing at her watch as she got up and went over to answer the insistent ringing of the phone. It was some unearthly hour in the morning . . . why had Sam let her sleep . . .

She repeated her name and the phone number . . . the faint voice that came floating over the wire was Muriel Grailey's . . . It was like sounds from another world — a world she had almost forgotten existed . . . but she was instantly awake . . . something must be seriously wrong for Muriel to ring her, particularly at this time of night . . . or rather, day . . . her heart quickened its beat as she listened . . .

'It's Tim — he's been injured in some kind of accident at Brand's Hatch, and they've taken him to hospital. I've only just got the news myself . . .'

'How serious is it?' Margaret's voice shook . . .

'I don't really know. It seems he's still unconscious. No bones are broken but they can't tell how serious the damage to his head is until he comes round . . . I wouldn't think it's exactly a matter of life or death, but I felt I should ring you directly I heard, and in any case, Linda's been phoning all over the place in an effort to find you, and of course as she couldn't trace you she's threatening to ring the police if I don't either tell her where you are, or contact you myself . . . '

Suddenly Margaret forgot everything except Tim and the fact that he had been hurt, that he might need her — nothing mattered but that. She had to get to him just as quickly as she could . . . at least now, she thought ruefully, perhaps her son would need her . . .

'I'll be home just as soon as I can arrange about trains and so on. Tell them at the hospital I'm on my way will you? And ask Linda if she'd take my Mini down to the garage in the village and get them to fill it with petrol and check the oil and so on so it's ready for me directly I arrive . . . '

Muriel repeated her instructions and rang off . . .

As Margaret replaced the receiver a cloud of misery, guilt and apprehension seemed to envelop her . . .

9

Sam drove Margaret to Plymouth to catch an early train next morning. As had been her arrival along the same road, it was a silent journey, each busy with their own thoughts . . .

Her mind was seething, bubbling like a cauldron with all the many problems which seemed to beset her now more than ever. She was remembering too, when John Beckett, the private detective she had hired to find her daughter — had driven her in the opposite direction — that too had been a silent trip as she wondered what she was going to find on her arrival at Queensbridge, what her daughter would be like.

And now she knew — had loved her and gone more than halfway along the road to winning her confidence and affection — and more important still, felt the girl herself, with her obvious love for Andy, was becoming established as a whole, independent, happy human being . . .

Really in a way Muriel's call and Tim's accident couldn't have come at a more inopportune time. Admittedly she felt a sense of guilt at having left the children so long without making sure for herself that all was well with them — she knew Muriel would shield her to a certain extent if she thought it was for her own good — and common sense told her that even if she had been at home, doubtless Tim would still have had the accident, still done exactly as he pleased, whatever she had advised.

She sighed, and hearing her, Sam put his hand on her knee.

He too had been lost in his own thoughts, wondering if this was good-bye to the woman he had grown to love and respect more than he had thought it possible for him to feel about anyone.

She was still an enigma, for although she had told him it was an urgent

213

family matter — a motor accident — and it was imperative she go — he knew no details or whether it was her intention ever to return to the Pack Horse . . .

'What are the odds against you coming back, lass?' He had to ask now, to be sure, with true Yorkshire forthrightness.

Margaret looked with unseeing eyes at the passing countryside, the shorn fields where the corn had been cut and carried — already at that early hour the sun was hot through the glass of the car window, no breeze lifted the leaves on the trees, and the cattle lay under the shade, chewing slowly at mouthfuls of withered grass . . . it had been a long hot summer . . . she could smell fresh tar, and late poppies nodded scarlet heads along the edge of the motorway, the hills of Dartmoor soft purple in the heat haze . . . she had grown to love Devon too in the short time she had been there — many things pulled at her heartstrings making her reluctant to face the journey ahead . . .

At last she said in answer to his query, 'I wish I knew, but I promise to get in touch with you directly I find out how things stand . . . '

'Leave me a phone number lass, just in case . . . ' he hesitated, feeling her eyes on him, 'well just in case anything should crop up — with Teresa say . . . '

She smiled at him now, thinking how transparent he was really under the tough outside. 'Yes, I'll do that, but you must promise really not to ring me unless it is absolutely vital. It could lead to . . . well . . . complications to say the least.'

He patted her knee, 'I promise, scout's honour . . . ' he tried a weak smile which didn't reach his eyes . . .

He parked the car, opened the door and took her case . . . when he found the platform and the waiting train, he got her a corner seat in the first class compartment for which he had insisted on getting the ticket . . . in spite of the circumstances, his rather proprietary

manner made her smile as he loaded
her down with magazines and a huge
box of chocolates . . .

'There's a diner a few coaches down,'
he stood uneasily on the platform
beneath the window, half tempted now
to get in beside her and to hell with the
consequences . . .

'Don't worry,' she gave his hand a
gentle squeeze . . . 'I can look after
myself, you go on back to the hotel, I
don't think you ought to ask too much
of Teresa just yet, and there are a lot of
breakfasts to serve this morning . . .
perhaps you'd explain to her why I've
had to go — I didn't have a chance and
I wouldn't like her to think . . . ' she
hesitated . . . 'well that I hadn't thought
about her . . . I'll let you know when
I'm coming back as soon as I can . . . '

The word 'when' instead of 'if'
brought him a little comfort, he pressed
her fingers, longing to take her in his
arms and kiss her . . . the train started
to move, doors banged, people shouted
. . . he turned and walked with hunched

shoulders back past the barrier and out on to the car park. Like a small child, he wouldn't let himself watch the train disappear from sight, in case it brought bad luck.

As for Margaret, watching the lonely figure, she felt a sudden rush of tears behind her eyelids — it was a familiar and endearing figure and she felt bereft, more alone than she ever remembered, although she was going back to her own home, her children, all her possessions, and the comfort that comparative wealth is supposed to bring . . .

The journey seemed to go on forever and somehow she felt even more alone when she arrived at the other end, although she had known no one would be at the station to meet her, she hadn't told Muriel the time of the train, she could get a taxi anyway, and she had an odd desire to put off as long as she possibly could, all the old familiar claims of her normal life . . . it seemed now that was the unnatural existence, and the one at the Pack Horse, the natural . . .

As the taxi swung into the drive she noticed the garden was as neat as ever, the beds bright with early autumn flowers, the fruit trees loaded with a shining harvest. Obviously her absence had made no difference to the smooth routine, but somehow she felt almost like a stranger, and it seemed a life time had passed since she had driven away from the house . . .

Muriel was standing on the steps to welcome her as the taxi drew up.

'Hope you had a good journey,' she said, as though Margaret had been to the city for a day's shopping.

Trust Muriel never to flap, never to pry, always to be on hand to comfort and help. What would she do without her . . .

But in spite of her outwardly casual attitude, Muriel's observation was none the less keen — and she had loved Margaret for many years as she might have a sister — she was sensitive to her every mood, every facet of her character . . .

She noticed she had thinned down — fined — was perhaps a better word. And in spite of the dark shadows under her eyes, occasioned probably by a sleepless night worrying about Tim — she had a radiance, an inner kind of tranquillity that had been missing before . . .

Margaret nodded in answer to her enquiry.

'Not too bad thanks. How's Tim? Is there any further news from the hospital? I think I'll have a quick bath and a change of clothes, and drive straight off — I won't bother with a meal . . .'

Muriel put out her hand as if to slow her down. 'There won't be any need. After I'd rung you the hospital themselves rang to say he'd be coming back this morning. He arrived a few minutes before you in fact, he's up in his room. I thought it best to make him go straight to bed, although he didn't want to of course. I took him a tray up to his room.' She paused, 'I didn't let you know because for one thing I thought you would have already left, and in any case I knew you'd rather come and see how things were for yourself . . . '

There was no hint of criticism in her voice, although Margaret had a feeling she deserved it . . .

She threw her hat and gloves on the hall chair and pushed the hair back from her forehead. 'You mean they sent him back by train?'

Now for some reason she wanted to delay the coming meeting with her son . . .

Muriel shook her head, 'No, his friend Nigel Stanford brought him, the one whose car he was driving when he had the accident. There's really not much wrong with him, apart from a gash on the head, which caused the concussion, and a broken wrist, but I gather he was unconscious rather longer than usual, and they were a bit anxious there might have been more damage than was apparent . . . '

Margaret went slowly towards the stairs. 'I'll go up then . . . '

Muriel followed her to the bottom of the stairs, and put her hand on her arm. 'Don't be surprised if you don't get a very enthusiastic reception! You're what they call in the doghouse with the two of them at the moment,' she smiled fleetingly. 'The young don't like their parents having secrets from them, it bruises their ego — the boot should be on the other foot, they consider secrecy really their own prerogative . . . '

Margaret grinned and patted the other woman's hand. 'I'm awfully grateful to you, in fact I just can't thank you enough for holding the fort, and beating off intruders! I've a lot to tell you, we'll have a cup of coffee when I've seen Tim — and a good natter . . . '

As she finished speaking the front door was flung open and Linda burst in.

Seeing her mother she stopped dead

in her tracks, her feet apart, her hands on her hips, looking at Margaret as if she were simply some unwelcome stranger in her home . . .

'So,' she said, 'you decided to come back at last . . .'

★ ★ ★

With difficulty Margaret choked back the angry words which rose to her lips. She gave her daughter a long, cool look . . .

'Naturally I came directly I heard Tim had had an accident and might need me, but although I haven't seen him yet, it appears he wasn't badly hurt after all.'

At that moment Tim's bedroom door opened and he came out in his dressing gown, his head swathed in bandages, one arm in a sling.

'I thought I heard voices, so our prodigal parent has returned to the fold!'

Margaret looked from one to the

other of them. 'Is this some kind of inquisition because whether it is or not, I find the whole thing very distasteful and extremely bad manners . . . '

Tim shrugged, looking abashed, Linda simply shifted from one foot to the other and looked slightly more sulky. 'Nope, not really, as a matter of fact we'd decided you'd pushed off for good, left us to the mercy of the Holy Grail.' It had been their childhood name for Muriel Grailey, one which Hugh had frowned upon but had not been able to suppress . . . Margaret was tempted in spite of the circumstances, to grin at the childish allusion . . .

'I don't intend to hold an inquest in the hall,' she said shortly, 'but if you'd both like to come into the drawing room, we'll discuss the situation like adults shall we? Muriel, perhaps you'd be kind enough to bring us some coffee,' she smiled at her, 'and then later you and I can have that chat we promised ourselves . . . '

Muriel was secretly overjoyed with

the way Margaret had handled the situation up to now — a few weeks ago she wouldn't have stood up to them like that. She smiled to herself, usually there was only one reason a woman gained extra confidence in herself, and it wasn't just through finding a lost daughter . . .

'I wonder what he's like,' she mused as she went through to the kitchen and put on the coffee to percolate. 'Probably I'll never know . . .'

In the drawing room, Margaret faced her inquisitors . . . Tim straddled the fireplace, looking so like his father that she had an overwhelming desire to laugh and smack his bottom . . . 'I would too if he was a few months younger,' she thought.

Linda had draped herself elegantly over a chair, one leg thrown over the arm, the inevitable cigarette between her fingers. 'I suppose it's better than pot,' she thought. Both she and Hugh had done their best to encourage the children never to start smoking — but as with everything else, they had gone their own sweet way . . .

'I suppose I did have a faint idea that my absence might have taught you a lesson at least to stop taking me for granted. But somehow I don't think it has. However that's beside the point.

'I must say I can't see quite what all the fuss is about, Muriel told me you intended ringing the police, Linda — did you imagine I'd been abducted or something?' she paused, 'not very likely at my age I think.'

'I did intend to get in touch with them,' Linda said coolly, 'it seemed the obvious thing to do when dear brother was hurt. I didn't of course know then that it was only a slight accident . . . it's like beating your head against a stone wall trying to get the truth out of a hospital sister on the other end of a telephone line . . . but I did think it only right you should be contacted . . . '

'Yes, you were quite right about letting me know, but all you had to do was tell Muriel, there was no need to make a three act drama out of it . . . '

'Well perhaps now you wouldn't mind telling us exactly where you have been,' Linda said.

Margaret glanced at Tim. He seemed temporarily to have lost his tongue. He always had been the more silent one of the pair, dominated by his forceful sister . . . 'and that's Hugh's spoiling, not mine,' she thought bitterly.

Unbidden, a picture of Teresa came into her mind as she looked at her younger daughter, her face a disagreeable mask of discontent and aggravation . . . Teresa — who had become so unbelievably dear in such a short time . . . so different from her stepsister — or was it half sister? She wasn't sure of the legal relationship — anyway it was almost ludicrous to couple them together . . .

Linda tapped her fingers on the arm of the chair, her eyebrows raised. If her whole attitude hadn't been so insolent, it would have been amusing, like a child aping its elders. All it needed was for her to say, 'Well — I'm waiting!'

'One thing I am going to make perfectly clear,' Margaret said slowly, 'I have no intention of telling you where I've been, it's entirely my own business, as I notice your movements usually are — I come and go as I please in my own home, the only person to whom I'm answerable is your father — and as he is out of the country at present there's no point in bothering him with my personal affairs.'

She paused, and then as she saw Linda was about to open her mouth again, she went on, 'And don't adopt that tone and attitude with me. If you must know, I've been helping an old friend, a very old friend, who was in difficulties,' she ended softly . . .

With hindsight she realised she'd handled the whole thing rather badly, too crudely — at the time it was partly because she hadn't thought that either Linda or Tim cared enough about what she did so long as it didn't interfere with their own lives and plans — to take any definite steps or make a move that might involve her. If she had, perhaps she would have approached the whole affair differently . . .

Now Linda got up and went towards the door. 'I imagine you'll be disappearing again now you know that Tim isn't in any danger . . . '

Margaret nodded, 'Very possibly. I'll get Doctor Ramsey to come and have a look at him, if he tells me there is nothing seriously wrong, then I do have some unfinished business to attend to . . . '

Without another word Linda went out of the front door, banging it behind her. They heard the engine of her Mini start up and a spurt of gravel as she drove away . . .

Now Tim smiled at her. 'Little sister does get aerated doesn't she? I'd be a bit worried if I was you, Mum. Those long painted nails are sharp as talons and so's that tongue.'

Margaret looked at him with surprise. She hadn't realised he'd suffered quite so much at his sister's hands as his tone indicated. Now she had been away and got things into true perspective, she could see how little she knew about her own children, really she knew Teresa better already than either of them with whom she'd been all their lives. Maybe it was because she had more sympathy with her — perhaps more in common even . . .

'I don't see that she can really do me much harm,' she said slowly.

Tim shrugged. 'I wouldn't bank on it. I've thought that in the past, to my cost . . .'

Doctor Ramsey came in answer to her phone call.

He gave Tim a thorough examination. 'Apart from the cuts and bruises, and that broken wrist, he's as fit as a fiddle,' he said, repacking his bag.

Then he turned swiftly, 'And you're looking better than I've seen you for a long time, Margaret.' He grinned. 'What's the secret of your success? A holiday in the sun?'

She laughed, feeling almost light-hearted for a moment, 'No, far from it really . . . Satisfaction I suppose, in achieving something I'd needed to do for a very long time . . . something that was perhaps colouring my life a shade of grey shall we say, and now I've come out of the clouds into the sunshine you mention, but rather a different kind . . . '

He turned back to his bag, shutting it with a snap. He'd been a doctor too long not to recognise a woman in love when he saw one. But he hoped she wouldn't lose her head and break up the family . . . he'd seen that happen all too often with women her age — and it had turned out in the end to be a whim, a passing fancy. But somehow he thought Margaret was much too sensible a woman, he had a great admiration for her and didn't think somehow she was the kind to go off the rails, as he put it . . .

'Hugh coming back soon?' he said cautiously.

She nodded, 'Yes, in the not too far distant future I think . . . '

'Good. Well, there's nothing better than a contented mind in a healthy body — a misquotation, but true all the same. Keep up the good work.

'As for that young man of yours, if I were him I'd choose less horses under the bonnet and take the corners a little more carefully. Next time he might not be so lucky . . . I wish you good day . . . '

When he'd gone Margaret said, 'You don't really want me here do you, Tim? I'll stay of course if you do, but I imagine you'll be off yourself again now . . . ' Her voice was just a little wistful, although she hadn't intended it to be.

He got up from the bed and put his arm round her shoulders, a gesture she'd long ago given up expecting.

'Thanks for coming Mum. It's nice to know you do care enough really.' He rubbed his chin on her shoulder, 'but I'm a big boy now, and the independent type as you know. There's a big race coming up in America in October. I've managed to get in on a package deal with some other chaps from the Motor Club — only fifty smackers in all — we leave here on the Thursday, New York for the night, might even call in and see Dad — then they run us out to the track for the practice on Saturday, the race on Sunday, and back on Monday, when we have a guided tour of the city in a heli . . . at that price it can't be bad . . . '

He kissed her briefly on the cheek.

'Please, Tim, be careful,' she said softly, 'in spite of what you may think, you are my son and very precious to me . . . both of you actually . . . '

She hadn't spoken to him like that for years, not since he was a small boy. For a moment she half expected a rebuff, or at the least, a burst of laughter. But he said:

'You go back to whatever it is you're doing, good or bad works! Enjoy yourself, and don't take too much notice of little sister. She'll grow up maybe, when she gets the right man to handle her!'

Margaret thought with a lightening of the heart that even if she had still to worry about Tim physically, there didn't seem to be too much wrong with him otherwise, he certainly didn't seem to suffer from what the young these days called hang ups, and she supposed at least motor racing was a healthy pastime in that it kept him out of doors and interested. One had to be thankful for small mercies ... and what a marvellous life they had, these children of the jet age — the Concorde age now perhaps — commuting backwards and forwards to Europe and America as if it were the next town ...

She sighed. If only she had been young now, Teresa certainly wouldn't have been a problem ... 'If only' ... perhaps the two saddest words in any language ...

She went down to the kitchen where Muriel was getting a late tea.

'I think I'll have a boiled egg, then I could perhaps catch the night train back to Plymouth,' Margaret said slowly.

The other woman kept her back turned. 'So you've decided to return to your . . . ' she paused a moment, and then added 'your friends?'

'Yes. I told the kids, I've some unfinished business . . . '

'Unfinished? You won't be staying for good then?'

Margaret sighed. 'I wish I knew . . . but no, I suppose not, all things considered . . .

She sat and slowly told Muriel about Teresa, about her own childhood, about Mike, about Tad and Andy . . .

Of Sam she spoke little — a fact which didn't escape Muriel's notice. She only mentioned him as her employer, avoiding the other's shrewd gaze . . . At the moment she couldn't bear the precious, vulnerable emotion that filled her whenever she thought of Sam, to have to withstand the harsh light of examination, of dissection by anyone else — not even Muriel, whom she loved perhaps as much as anyone . . . she just wanted to cherish it, to hug it to herself alone . . .

Muriel broke in on her thoughts, 'One night isn't going to hurt,' she said shortly. 'And you'd do better sleeping in your own bed than in some dirty train. I'll find out the times you can leave in the morning, and arrange a taxi . . . then you can let your . . . ' she paused again a moment, 'your friends know what time to meet you at the other end . . . '

And so it was arranged, and now it was an accomplished fact, Margaret was impatient to return to the Pack Horse. She told herself it was natural anxiety to make sure everything was running smoothly, to see Teresa again — but in her heart she knew it was more than that. She was missing Sam bitterly — with his blunt, wholesome outlook — and the feeling of being needed, cherished . . .

She put through a call to the hotel from her bedroom extension, making sure Tim was safely in his room.

When she'd dialled she waited with mounting excitement, just like a lovesick schoolgirl, to hear Sam's voice . . . her heart beat so loudly she was sure it would be apparent to him the other end . . .

But it was Teresa who answered . . . it was a moment of anticlimax in a way, but it was lovely to hear the girl's voice, confident, self assured . . . 'Everything's going fine Mrs Smith,' Teresa said, 'I'm afraid Mr Perrett isn't in at the moment. He had to go down to the suppliers — but I'll tell him the time of the train so he can meet you . . . it'll be lovely to see you back,' she added softly . . .

And Margaret wondered if he'd mentioned her name to Teresa, what he'd said and how much he'd missed her in the few hours they'd been apart . . .

10

When she first awoke the next morning she couldn't think for the moment where she was.

She had got so used to the tiny room at the Pack Horse, to the sounds coming in from the main street of the market town that she found the comparative silence and peace of the surrounding country, the vague outlines of unfamiliar furniture, all strange.

Muriel brought her morning tea — a luxury she'd almost forgotten . . . and as she drew back the curtains and let the early autumn sun stream in, bringing the scent of late roses, she said, 'It's going to be a beautiful day, sky's blue as a delphinium petal — pity you can't stay a while and relax in the garden, it's really looking beautiful this year . . .'

Margaret had to smile. 'You are

waxing lyrical, Muriel, I never knew you were a poet!'

'There's a great deal we never know — even suspect — about each other,' the woman said, rather curtly for her, but she softened the words with a smile. 'I'll have your breakfast ready in twenty minutes, that'll give you time for a shower. I've put out fresh clothes and packed your cases again . . . still the small one. I take it that's in order.'

Her tone hinted at the fact that Margaret's destination was possibly some uncivilised foreign country . . .

It was odd to have everything done for her, not to be the one who did the planning, the waiting, the organising — she had to admit it was enjoyable, but would she ever be able to settle again to this useless, aimless existence — where she really wasn't needed, had no function to perform?

She shrugged off the thought for the moment, 'I'll think about that tomorrow,' she told herself . . .

And in fact a light hearted and

carefree mood filled her once again as she got into the taxi and waved goodbye to Muriel. She had thought of taking the Mini, but changed her mind — was it because she knew Sam liked the feeling of dependence on him the fact that she had no transport of her own gave? Maybe ... She chided herself briefly for having become so Sam orientated ...

There was no sign of Linda, and Tim had told her goodbye last night for he had to be off very early in the morning, hoping to hitch a lift to the continent on one of the lorries that passed on the motorway to the roll on roll off ferry — it meant leaving before dawn ...

She settled back in the carriage with a sigh of content. At least for the time being she had straightened things out at home, and there was still quite a bit of time before Hugh was due to return — before she had to face the decision which she was finding it more and more difficult to face up to ...

Maybe if she had seen Linda slipping

the pale blue air mail letter into the pillar box in the village, and caught sight of the name on the envelope, she wouldn't have been quite so complacent — now all she could think about was the immediate future — and Teresa and Sam — my adopted family, she thought with a grin.

He was waiting at the station, impatient as a young lover.

This time he kissed her gently on the mouth, not caring who saw. He took her case from her, and holding her arm, guided her to the car, as if half fearful she would escape him again . . .

He'd ordered lunch in an expensive and exclusive restaurant in the city, and insisted she drink some wine, although she protested she never did such a thing at lunch time . . .

'This is an occasion, Maggie. I thought I'd lost you, but you've come back to me . . . '

She looked at him over the rim of her glass. 'It's only a St Martin's Summer, Sam. Please don't let yourself think anything different . . . '

He looked ruffled for the moment. 'O.K. if you say so, but I need you Maggie, Teresa needs you too. We missed you like hell, both of us . . . ' He paused, 'But the kid did a grand job, I'll say that, took over like a veteran, cool as a cucumber. Think I may give her your job when you go . . . '

He didn't look at her, throwing out the words as a challenge . . . Margaret put down her glass now . . . her eyes glowing with pleasure . . .

'Sam that would be wonderful. Do you really mean it? It's just what she needs — that and Andy Rossiter.'

For a moment he was piqued.

'She's all you think about isn't she, lass? How about poor old Sam?' He took her hands in both his, she let them rest for a moment, enjoying the warm feeling that ran up the nerves of her arms . . . then she said . . .

'Anyone less in need of sympathy than 'poor old Sam' would be hard to imagine — and I do think about you, more than you know perhaps . . . but you'll manage, you always have and you always will again, people like you and I do. Think of me just as an inter-lude . . . '

'I'm damned if I will!' he raised his voice so that the people at the next table looked at them with amused glances. Margaret felt herself go red as she quickly withdrew her hands from his grasp.

'Sam! What will people think?'

He gazed round belligerently, more like a bull terrier than ever. 'I don't care a blooming fig what they think,' he blustered, 'you're the best thing that ever happened to me and I don't care who knows it . . . '

'Then let's not argue. Enjoy your lunch, it's costing you enough,' she smiled at him disarmingly, and slightly mollified he had to give a rueful laugh.

'You know how to get round me, lass, twist me right round your finger, and I reckon that girl of yours is going to take after you, got a real way with her now she's lost that chip she seemed to carry round.'

'That's through knowing someone cares,' she said slowly, 'and you can help there by giving her responsibility, like you suggested.' She sipped her wine. 'Has she seen anything of Andy since I've been away?'

He grinned again. 'What a broody old hen you are! You've only been gone a matter of hours and you expect her to have trapped the young cockerel already . . . well as a matter of fact they've been out to dinner, and I believe they have another date for tomorrow — satisfied?'

She nodded. 'Yes, perfectly . . . '

The rest of the meal they talked of the Pack Horse, of the improvements he had thought of and she had suggested, and of the season just passed.

She was relieved that from then on the conversation was on a more impersonal level, at the moment she was so uncertain, confused about her own future, she needed a respite to think, to plan . . .

Teresa was enchantingly pleased to see her. With a lift of the heart Margaret realised she was hardly recognisable as the same girl she had been a few weeks ago when she'd first arrived at the Pack Horse with John Beckett . . .

Now she took great care with her appearance, her face was beautifully but sparingly made up, her hair neat and shining, and she was wearing a simple grey dress with white collar and cuffs that Margaret had helped her to make.

I'll make a point of telling Sam what an obvious asset she's going to be, she thought, a little smile curving her lips. With a charming naturalness, Teresa lifted her face for Margaret's kiss, and inevitably she felt a sharp pang of regret as she compared this welcome with the one she had had from Linda . . .

She resolved to waste no time in pressing her ideas for Teresa, and rather grudgingly Sam agreed she should give up waiting in the dining room to train as manageress, working with Margaret all the time . . . she explained to the girl that her own position had always been on a temporary basis, that Mr Perrett had been looking for someone suitable to take her place, and that she had amply proved herself capable of being that someone.

Teresa's face glowed.

'Do you really think I shall be able to manage? It's different when you're here,' she looked a little doubtful, 'I mean I can always come to you with my troubles and problems, and you always understand — you're always so kind, like over Tad . . . I'm not sure about Mr Perrett, I sometimes feel he doesn't really like me, although I must say he's been ever so kind while you've been away . . . ' her face coloured and she looked down at her hands . . .

'Nonsense.' Margaret smiled at her, 'I'm quite sure he likes you — he's as good as told me so — it was simply that he thought perhaps you had got in with rather bad company — and after all he didn't know much about you — just as he didn't about me for that matter . . . '

'You mean the Tad business?'

Margaret nodded . . .

'Yes, he was a bit of a mistake, poor Tad,' the girl said slowly, 'but I suppose most of us make some kind of mess of growing up . . . even you perhaps.'

Margaret glanced at her quickly, but her face was expressionless.

'That's a certain fact,' Margaret said, 'and I don't even know that I have learnt much better now, in spite of my age.'

They smiled at each other like fellow conspirators and Teresa said, 'I can't believe that, you're so capable, so assured, it's easy to see you know how to deal with any kind of situation that arises.'

'I wish I could believe you,' Margaret said drily, then she went on, 'I read the other day, talking about some kind of crisis a young person had been through, that experience is just part of the rich fabric that is life . . . I suppose that's true, for both young and old, it would be a dull pattern if there were no dark patches to highlight the bright ones — so I think we'll have to try looking at things that way . . . '

Now they spent most of the working day together, and to Margaret's secret joy, Andy invited Teresa over to the farm, or out for a meal or a dance with the Young Farmers' Club every free moment she had — and in many ways she managed to wangle the girl plenty of free time . . . She seemed to have endeared herself to the whole Rossiter family, and so with a sigh, Margaret had to admit to herself at last that her job at the Pack Horse was nearly completed in all its facets . . . she had accomplished what she set out to do, and it would only be fair to give Sam a definite deadline for when she would have to leave . . .

And yet she kept putting it off, torn between this feeling she had for him, her interest in Teresa's future, and the years of marriage to Hugh — precious in their many memories, in the ties that bound through children, all the hard times, the sorrows and joys they'd lived through together . . . and which she knew could never be repeated or replaced by anyone else . . .

It was a sad yet compelling decision she had to make . . .

Meanwhile she helped Teresa to find and interview another young girl to act as waitress so she could devote all her time to learning the office work and the hundred other jobs entailed in running a small country hotel . . .

She got on well with the rest of the staff, there seemed to be no resentment from Joe or the cook that she was taking over the reins from Margaret, young as she was — and the older woman heaved a sigh of relief for she had been afraid this might have led to troubled relationships . . . but perhaps because of her own somewhat unhappy child-hood, Teresa seemed to have a sympathy, a knack of handling other people . . . maybe that's one good legacy I have given her, Margaret thought ruefully.

On the whole life was running smoothly and pleasantly. Muriel had rung to say all was quiet at home, for the moment, anyway. Tim had phoned from America to say he was safe and well and enjoying himself, and Linda was in and out as she always was, restless, unsettled, but not seemingly any different from usual . . .

Margaret had decided she would give herself just two more weeks before she went home — then she would have time to settle in and resume the cloak of her marriage, before Hugh returned . . .

It was a few evenings later, as she sat at dinner with Sam before the dining room actually opened for visitors, that Teresa came in from the office, she looked flustered — an unusual occurrence for her nowadays . . .

'There's a gentleman asking for you Mrs Smith . . . he won't wait, although I told him you were having dinner, and that if it was a booking, I'd deal with it,' she hesitated, 'actually he asked for a

Mrs Gennert and it took some time for me to realise who he meant . . . I think he thought I was very stupid . . . I'm sorry . . . I hope I haven't upset things for you. I did tell him I couldn't possibly disturb you, but he wouldn't take no for an answer . . . '

Before Margaret could recover her senses, or get to her feet — a man strode across the dining room and she started to shake uncontrollably as she looked up into Hugh's furious face, and accusing eyes . . .

11

Sam took in the situation at once — in fact in the back of his mind he'd been anticipating something of the kind . . . he sent Teresa off into the kitchen on some pretext over dinner — then taking Margaret gently by the arm, he led her across to the office, brushing past Hugh, saying firmly, 'Perhaps you would be good enough to follow us . . . ' which, surprisingly he did, the torrent of words which had been on his lips temporarily silenced by Sam's obvious air of authority . . .

For all their sakes he was anxious to get the two of them safely into the office, the door firmly closed, before the storm, which he knew was inevitable, should break in all its fury . . . Above all he knew Margaret would not want Teresa to hear what Hugh was about to say, for although he didn't know the full story, he had a pretty shrewd idea of the gist of it . . .

He herded them into the small office and then shut the door behind them, standing for a moment on the outside, wishing there was more he could do . . . but he knew they must be left for the time being . . . he turned and went into the bar, ordering a stiff brandy, which he drank neat at one gulp . . .

Meanwhile Hugh was leaning against the closed door, looking at Margaret. Some of the steam seemed to have gone out of him as she gazed back at him . . .

'I . . . ' he began, floundering now for words, 'I . . . perhaps first I should explain my reasons for being here, and how and why . . . although most of the explaining is going to have to be done by you,' he said shortly.

'I had thought for some time it was odd I had had so few, and such scrappy letters from you . . . then Linda sent me an airmail after Tim's accident,' he paused for a moment, 'she didn't of course tell me where you'd gone as she said you had told no one — but Sybil Seymour saw my car pass the village hall as I drove from the airport as luck would have it, and she came on up to the house to ask if you'd be back to help with the Autumn Fair, or something . . . it was then she told me she'd seen you here — she was certain it was you, although you put up some feeble pretence not to know her . . . ' he paused for breath, then broke out. 'In God's name, Margaret, what kind of game are you playing?'

The first thing that occurred to Margaret at his words, was what rotten luck it was that Sybil had seen her that day in the dining room — some women would have had the decency to keep their mouths shut — and yet as she stood facing Hugh at last, seeing the lines that anxiety had etched on his face, a great flood of compassion, of love and warmth towards him, flowed through her . . .

It was true she had been very attracted to Sam — could easily have fallen in love with him had things been different — even had a little, she admitted — but now she knew her feelings had been in some strange way an indirect result of missing Hugh, of being separated from him, all she had felt for Sam she had once felt for her husband.

The events of the past few weeks seemed to have eclipsed that love, but now she felt it again — strong — waiting once more to burst into flower, perhaps more strongly than ever . . .

But now she knew she had to tell him something which might be even more painful than the situation which he had envisaged — that she was having an affair with Sam . . .

It was just that the actual moment of showdown had come earlier than she had anticipated but she had known it must come, and maybe in a way as a surprise was better than having to think it all out in cold blood . . .

All these years she'd carried an

overpowering burden of guilt and remorse . . . she knew now she should have shared that burden with him, as now they shared the agony in this moment of truth . . .

Maybe I've been the wrong wife for him, she thought, but she couldn't help remembering the good times, the times of joy — mostly before they'd been quite so well off . . .

Now he stood waiting for her to speak, to give him her explanation . . .

'I . . . ' she drew a deep breath, 'I don't know how I'm going to tell you this — but please try to understand, to forgive me . . . and to be patient.

'I've tried to share your troubles in the past — I know I haven't always been successful — but I have tried . . . please come to meet me half-way now,' she pleaded. 'Things aren't in the least what you think . . . ' She felt as if she were fighting for her life which, perhaps in a way, she was . . .

He made a gruff sound which could have meant anything . . .

'Before I met you there was someone else,' she sank into a chair so she could take her eyes off his face while she told him, unable to meet the expression which might show in his . . .

'In fact what I'm trying to tell you — after twenty years of marriage — is that you were not the first man I slept with . . . '

Now the actual bare facts in words were out, she had a curious sensation. It was of shame, as if she'd taken off all her clothes in a public place and now stood naked before him . . .

But at the same time it was as if an enormous burden had been lifted from her — a marvellous feeling of relief from tension . . .

He lifted his hand in an instinctive gesture, as if to ward off a blow.

When he spoke his voice was so low she could scarcely hear the words . . . 'I wondered . . . the way you behaved sometimes — you were so strange, so withdrawn . . . I thought you simply didn't love me any more — and yet I

256

didn't think there was anyone else — felt I would have known ... I couldn't imagine what had changed between us, where the feeling, the closeness that we'd once had, had gone ... '

She nodded, 'Perhaps it was just because of that we grew apart ... maybe it was I who made you undemonstrative ... '

'I've always loved you from the first, there was never anyone else for me,' he went on softly ...

'You scarcely even kissed me — a peck on the cheek, not the mouth, when you got home from the office ... you never shared your day, communicated with me ... you took me for granted as part of the fabric of your life — the background to what really mattered — and the kids took that pattern for their own behaviour ... I felt that none of you really needed me — while I knew, felt certain, that somewhere there was someone who did ... '

'So,' he said slowly as she stopped, 'it wasn't another man I was fighting — there was something else, someone else . . . a child . . . and all these years you've shared my life, my bed, my home — you've been living a double life, deceiving me . . . '

He sank into a chair and covered his face with his hand, his whole body shaking with shock and anger.

For a moment Margaret watched him. She ached with compassion for him, it was like a physical pain . . .

She got up and knelt down beside him, gently drawing his head down on to her breast, talking quietly, soothingly, as if to a child . . .

'I know it looks like that, but I didn't mean it to be. I couldn't bear at first to lose your good opinion of me — you always told me I was so different from the other girls you knew — innocent — how could I destroy that? Then, as the years passed it became more and more difficult, more impossible to bring up the subject . . . '

'But I still can't see why you're here with that man . . . your lover I suppose — father of the child . . . '

She shook her head. 'Sam is only incidental, he means nothing to me,' she said slowly, knowing she must deny any feeling for him now to save her marriage . . . 'it's that Teresa, my daughter — works here. A private detective found her for me, and I came to get a job so I could be near her, try to help her, to repay some of the enormous debt I owe . . . it seemed the least I could do . . . '

Slowly she got to her feet, wondering if she'd got through to him at all . . . he still sat gazing into space. He was trying to come to terms with this Margaret he had never known . . .

There were so many things he remembered now — how she seemed gradually to have grown away from him, her sadness at times for no apparent reason, times when she had been withdrawn, distant, as if she were living in a past in which he had no place — now it was all so clear, so different from what he had imagined . . .

Gradually he began to see what she must have gone through, how she must have felt — suffering the torment of the very devil, wondering about the child, longing to see her, and having no one she could confide in . . .

Margaret had gone over to the desk and lit a cigarette — a thing she rarely if ever did . . . she didn't know why she had now, it was just she had to occupy her hands . . . the smoke made her cough . . . at that moment Sam knocked on the door, and she called 'Come in . . . '

He'd waited for a moment in the hall when he came from the bar — but there was no sound of voices raised in anger as he feared there might be — or had he secretly hoped — when he realised this was Margaret's husband — hoped there would be a final showdown of some kind, that at last she might turn to him for comfort . . . No, if he was honest he didn't wish that on her, even for himself . . .

Hugh got to his feet as Sam entered the room . . .

'This is Sam Perrett — my husband — Hugh Gennert,' Margaret said.

Sam held out his hand. Hugh took it and held it for a moment . . .

'Forgive me Mr Perrett, I'm afraid over in the dining room I was rather rude, I owe you an apology, I misunderstood the situation, jumped to a wrong conclusion, Margaret has made it all clear to me now . . . '

Sam nodded briefly.

'Forgotten soon as asked,' he said abruptly, 'but I feel I must say this, Mr Gennert, though I have no right at all, but however things turn out I envy you, you are a lucky man — you have a wonderful wife, a woman in a million . . . '

For a moment Hugh stood looking at him. Sam wondered, watching the conflict of emotions on his face, if this tall, powerful man were about to strike him, he didn't know what Margaret might have told him . . . but he only said quietly:

'Thank you Mr Perrett, I agree with you, although I think it's taken me rather a long time to come to that conclusion . . . you are perfectly correct, Margaret is a wonderful person . . .'

★   ★   ★

Hugh still felt stunned by all that had passed in the few short moments he had been with Margaret . . . but he had no alternative but to leave after she'd got him a tray of food and some coffee. His plane left from London Airport early the next morning.

'It's annoying, but I still have some unfinished business in New York, which Linda's letter interrupted . . . I suppose I can't persuade you to come with me?' he held her hand in both his . . .

She shook her head. 'No, I too have a little unfinished business,' she smiled at him. 'In all the excitement I had forgotten that Teresa and Andy have got engaged — I think they are hoping to get married before too long, apparently his parents don't like long engagements, with which I agree wholeheartedly — I promised I'd come back for a few days to supervise the reception and so on . . . also she wants to make her own dress and some of her trousseau, so we have a great deal of shopping to do . . . and I want to make quite sure she is ready to take over here when I go — there are a few loose ends to tie up . . . '

Tactfully Sam had left them alone while Hugh ate his meal, and Margaret had tried, in the time they had, to tell him the whole story — not only of her life before she had met him — only part of which he knew — and also of the long years between — years of sunshine and shadow, and of Muriel's love and devotion — and ultimately of her decision to find the daughter she had never known and lay forever, the shadow from the past ... of her contacting John Beckett and how swiftly he had worked on her behalf ... 'and that explains the mysterious withdrawal of cash,' he smiled as he drank the last of the coffee ...

Margaret nodded. Teresa had brought them the meal on trays and Margaret had introduced Hugh as her husband, saying no more about the fact that Smith was not her name, for the time being she would leave the girl to draw her own conclusions — domestic troubles, a tiff, which she could obviously see had been settled now ...

And Hugh had gazed at Teresa, trying to keep the curiosity and surprise from his face, thinking too, 'She might have been my daughter ... ' and wishing in a way Margaret had decided to tell the girl the truth ... at first he had been inclined to insist that she should, that Teresa should leave the Pack Horse and come home with them, be integrated into the family — but at last Margaret had swayed him by her arguments and grudgingly he had had to admit she was probably right . . .

As the time came to part, they kissed almost as young lovers would, she felt as if the old days of their courtship had returned as she went to the car to see him off. He held her hand, reluctant to let this new found love go, even for a couple of weeks.

'You haven't got an easy task ahead,' he said softly, smiling up at her from the driving seat, 'to have to choose the wedding clothes for your own daughter under the guise of only friendly interest must be about the most difficult job a woman can be asked to do . . . '

She bent and kissed him gently on the cheek, the familiar smell of the expensive after shave he used sent a little thrill along her nerves.

'It won't be nearly so difficult now, knowing I have your love and support behind me,' she said softly . . .

He started the engine, 'Only two weeks, then I'll be back and we'll go away for a few days eh? Scotland's lovely in September — a second honeymoon, without having to worry if we have enough cash to settle the bill, like we did on the first one!'

She felt tears prick behind her lids as she watched the tail light of the car disappear up the street. It was difficult to believe so much had happened in so few hours — she had lived a lifetime of torment, uncertainty, confession and then sweet joy and relief in a matter of hours. Now she felt spent, drained of all emotion as she turned back and went slowly up the steps into the inn.

If Teresa was curious as to what all the fuss and secrecy had been about, she didn't ask — Margaret explained briefly that she and Hugh had had a bit of a tiff — a domestic upset, as married people of their age did sometimes —

'I came away rather suddenly as I am sure you must have guessed,' Margaret said, 'hoping to clear up my problems,' well that was true enough for certain, 'sometimes,' she went on, 'it is easier to get things in proper perspective from a distance, and I'm glad to say that both my husband and I have done so, and I think I can say that everything is smoothed out again.'

Teresa smiled at her, a thing she did often lately, specially since she had spoken of her coming engagement — Margaret was amused to see the smile was tinged with a little indulgence now as if she were the elder and Margaret the younger — so wise was she about love now!

'I'm so glad, although I think Mr Perrett has a very soft spot for you,' she blushed, wondering then if she'd been too bold, a little too familiar.

To her relief Margaret burst out laughing. 'Oh well I suppose even we old folks have our 'fancies' sometimes, but usually we're sensible and experienced enough to realise there really isn't any institution yet invented that's better than marriage, and when one has spent half a lifetime with one person, it's difficult to imagine a change. There are so many little things — and big ones — that you've shared over the years that no one else could possibly begin to understand or replace . . . I'm sure you'll find that out . . . '

Teresa nodded wisely, giving her one of her spontaneous hugs. 'I'm so glad it's all worked out for you — and me — you're the kind of person that just deserves the best — always . . . '

For a moment Margaret felt a shadow on her happiness . . . 'I wonder what you'd think if you really knew . . . '

Together they bought white velvet for the dress, for it was to be a Christmas wedding in the little country church near the Rossiter farm where all the family had been married, christened and buried for nearly three hundred years . . .

'It has got an ancient stove, but it's still frightfully cold,' Teresa grinned, 'and I'd rather be warm than a pale blue with cold, that's why I thought velvet would be better than satin . . . '

There were to be two bridesmaids,

cousins of Andy's, they were going to wear scarlet velvet and carry posies of Christmas roses, the same as Teresa's bouquet, all from Mrs Rossiter's beloved garden . . .

'I know it's months away, but I'm so excited already I think I shall burst before the day actually comes,' the girl said as they cut and pinned and tacked, in a frenzy of activity before Margaret had to leave — all in between seeing to the guests and trying to keep Sam from treading on material and paper patterns which seemed to litter every square inch of ground . . .

Margaret had said she would like to buy the dress and most of the trousseau as a wedding present . . .

'But you can't — it's too much . . .' Teresa protested, her eyes shining. Then she said softly, 'Although I never knew my mother — and I know of course she couldn't really have been the slightest bit like you, or she'd never have let me go, I like to dream, to hope even, she might have been something like if — well if things had been different . . . '

Before she could stop herself a sob escaped from Margaret's lips. Quickly she took out her handkerchief and blew her nose. The girl looked at her.

'Are you O.K.? Not starting a cold or anything? There's an awful lot of 'flu about . . . '

Margaret gave her a watery smile. 'No, I'm just being silly, it's the wedding and all the excitement, typically female, it brings tears to my eyes . . . but I'd be proud if you could feel I have in a way replaced the mother you never knew,' she hesitated. 'Maybe she wasn't as bad as you think, things were so different when you were born — society frowned on girls having babies when they weren't married — if it happened today perhaps she would have kept you . . . '

The girl nodded and said slowly, 'I hadn't thought of it that way, maybe you're right. As I'm so happy, and things have turned out so well, let's forgive her shall we?' She smiled up at Margaret.

Hardly trusting herself to speak, she said, 'Yes, let's do just that, and we've done enough for today, let's go and have a glass of sherry before dinner. We deserve it . . . and poor Mr Perrett too — he has a lot to put up with without a couple of females ganging up on him!'

12

The days flew by on winged feet — saying goodbye was painful for all three of them, only tempered by the knowledge she would be back . . . but Sam couldn't hide the fact that it felt like the end of the world . . . as the train took her further and further away she too felt a deep sadness, a nostalgia for their time together . . .

It was impossible not to compare this second homecoming with the last, so short a time ago . . . the garden still looked as though it had been carefully manicured, but now the roses had been replaced by dahlias and chrysanthemums and the leaves were turning on the trees . . .

Hugh and I could manage this garden between us — together — she thought suddenly as the taxi bore her up the drive . . . dispense with the gardener and do it all ourselves — even if it doesn't look quite so perfect, at least it'll be all our own work, a shared interest. We'll go in for roses, spend the evenings studying catalogues and sprays, blackspot and greenfly . . . she giggled to herself at the picture this conjured up. But why not? Maybe now, with this new understanding between them, Hugh would be able to spend less time at the office, surely now he could delegate some of the work . . .

Linda was in the hall, behind Muriel, as she opened the door.

Margaret felt a moment's apprehension . . . she'd almost forgotten, she had this to deal with still . . . this antagonism . . .

But the usual sulky expression she had grown to expect, had been ironed out, replaced by an almost shy smile as she kissed her mother warmly, running into her arms as she had done as a child . . .

'Nice to have you back in the old ancestral,' she said, her tone and words

273

flip — but her eyes pleaded . . . 'Please don't misunderstand me — I've changed, I want to be friends . . . forget what I was like and try to understand — I am your daughter . . . '

Tea was laid in the long low sitting room with the french windows open wide to the garden and the perfume still lingering in the beds, filled the warm air. Margaret flopped down and kicked off her shoes . . .

'It's good to be home . . . '

Muriel poured the tea. 'I don't ever remember hearing you say that before!'

Margaret smiled at them. 'Being away teaches one to appreciate one's own perhaps,' she said slowly.

Linda glanced at her quickly. 'That goes for people too, when they're gone you miss them, realise how much you'd taken them for granted — when it could be too late . . . '

If that's a plea for a new relationship, then you shall have it, Margaret thought as she sipped her tea, but she wondered what could have brought about such a quick change of heart. Surely not just her absence.

Anyway Linda had always been her father's girl — not her mother's . . .

Suddenly an idea struck her. That could be it. It was her father she had been thinking of — the fact that Margaret had gone off with some other man would deeply hurt her father — that could well be the explanation . . . but it would have to come from the girl herself — she mustn't probe . . . that might destroy the delicate new relationship — tender as a seedling . . .

The talk was general as the three women ate their tea — of local happenings in the village, Hugh's return from America, the suggested plan for a holiday in Scotland . . .

'How about you Linda, would you like to join us?' Margaret asked.

The girl got up and came over to sit beside her mother. As if on cue, Muriel picked up the tea tray.

'Back to the sink for me,' she smiled, 'I've had my holiday and I can't say I'll be sorry to have the house full up again — it's been a lonely place these last weeks.'

Margaret smiled at her. 'It's nice to be missed, anyway . . . '

As the woman went out, closing the door behind her, Linda said softly, 'You can say that again . . . ' She turned her eyes, which were so like Hugh's, to Margaret, and said impulsively . . .

'I'm sorry, Mum — about everything — writing to Dad, and that vile Seymour woman — I didn't mean it to turn out like it did,' she hesitated . . .

Margaret put out her hand and stroked the silky hair, 'I know, love, but not to worry, you did as you thought best and it's all turned out O.K. I was largely to blame for the way I handled the situation, I should have realised — known better — it was just that I had to do something — ' she hesitated, wondering how best to put it, 'to justify myself perhaps is the best way of explaining — to right a wrong I did many years ago — to the best of my ability anyway. Something inside me wouldn't be satisfied until I tried to make amends . . . and that made me difficult to live with, I realise that now . . . '

The girl bent forward and traced a ladder down her nylon clad leg, making it an excuse to hide her face behind the curtain of hair . . .

'Dad and I had a long talk when he came home — before he went down to Devon to find you actually . . . ' Margaret let out a long sigh of relief, for one moment she thought Linda meant Hugh had told her about Teresa, then she realised he would never break a confidence . . . Linda went on, 'you see I thought you'd gone off with someone else — those mysterious phone calls, then disappearing into the blue directly Dad had left — and I couldn't bear him to be hurt — then I found too that I couldn't bear to have you gone either . . . I realised I'd been a selfish pig — taking all you did for me for granted . . . '

Impulsively now she lifted her face to be kissed . . . 'and I can't possibly believe you ever needed to right any wrong you'd done in the past, you just don't have it in you to be mean . . . '

I wonder why everyone thinks that about me, Margaret thought to herself, I suppose it only proves how little we know the people we live with . . . she longed to be able to tell Linda about Teresa, but for the time she knew she couldn't . . . perhaps later when she and Hugh had talked it all over again at leisure — but not now, for now she would just enjoy the new found relationship with her daughter — my younger daughter — she thought with a little smile . . .

'How's Tim?' she asked now as Linda got up to switch on the news . . .

'Oh fine, he'll be home tomorrow. As a matter of fact we were thinking of making up a foursome to go to Majorca on one of those package deals while you and Dad are away. We wouldn't dream of intruding on you two lovebirds!' she grinned at her mother.

'Be honest, you'd both be bored to tears, I've no doubt we shall spend the whole time saying, 'do you remember . . . ?' It's the favourite phrase of the middle aged!'

Linda sat again on the arm of the sofa and swung her legs . . .

'You're neither of you middle aged — there's no such thing these days — anyway it's how you feel inside. I admit Dad's got a bit of a tum, but nothing some golf won't iron out, and a few less expense lunches!' she laughed . . . then went on, 'I know just the colour hair tint that would suit you, Mum, take years off, specially with the new coloured lipsticks now in fashion . . . I'll get one next time I go into town.'

She got up, 'Must fly, I'm playing tennis with Letty and Pam at six.' She bent and kissed her mother on the cheek, her lips lingering for a moment as she fluttered her eyelashes against the soft skin in what they had called as children a 'butterfly kiss' . . . for a moment Margaret felt a pang of remorse, of divided loyalties as she remembered Teresa and her remarks as they sewed her wedding dress . . .

She sighed, if only she could bring them all together — but it just wasn't possible yet. You couldn't change the past and in any case she was pretty certain that if she did tell Teresa who she was, the girl wouldn't want to become part of a family she had never known and not grown up as part of . . . things were best left as they were, a compromise perhaps, but life was one long compromise and she'd never forget the bitter outburst over Tad that Teresa had made that day in the caravan . . .

* * *

It only took a few days to readjust and settle back into the old routine at home — although now it had a different appeal and her heart was in it more than it had ever been. They all went to the airport to meet Hugh's plane — a united family once more and he seemed more relaxed and cheerful than she had seen him for years . . . the next day the two children went off on their Majorcan holiday and Margaret and Hugh put the car on the motorail for Scotland . . . in a way it was as if the Pack Horse and Queensbridge and all it meant had never been . . . and yet things had changed beyond her wildest dreams . . .

The days flew by on wings, in the small hotel Hugh looked at her across the breakfast table, through the window they could see down the glen to where the loch sparkled in the October sunshine . . . the sky was blue and cloudless and both of them were tanned from the golf they'd been playing, and the walks they'd taken over the heather clad hills . . .

He squeezed her hand, not caring who saw that he loved his wife.

'You're more lovely than you were as a bride,' he said softly.

She laughed. 'Flatterer! It's the light up here in the hills, it seems to have a quality you don't get in England — not near London anyway . . . '

He shook his head. 'No, it's nothing to do with the outside — it's from within, for both of us I think. We've learnt the hard way, and it's taken time, but thank God we did learn before it was too late. At least I've come to realise you are a person in your own right, with your own life to lead, and not someone I had come to take for granted — what an ignorant oaf I've been, wasting all those years . . . '

'Linda said much the same to me,' she answered gently, 'and from the bottom of my heart I thank you both for that . . . '

Now he pushed back his chair and got to his feet. 'Well, it's back to the grindstone on Monday I suppose. Still I'm taking your advice and easing off, we'll go along to those Nurseries we saw today, and order the roses you fancy. They say there are no roses like the Scottish ones, must be something to do with the climate — the survival of the fittest! Although we can't complain about the weather we've been treated to . . . '

She burst out laughing. 'You'd better not let any of the Scots hear you say that or they'll hack you to pieces with their claymores or dirks or whatever! They hold a pretty high opinion of their weather . . . '

As they went across the hall of the hotel he glanced at himself in the mirror.

'I really believe I've lost a few inches round the middle with all this unaccustomed exercise you've driven me to, woman!'

He rested his arm along her shoulders. 'I shall have to order a new suit for the wedding — I think I may even have a grey morning affair, might as well be in fashion, and that seems to be what the young man about town favours these days,' he paused, 'and would do for Ascot next year, I think we might as well splash out and enjoy ourselves a bit, Meg — how about a box eh?'

She drew his arm round her neck and looked up at him, serious for a moment, she couldn't remember when he'd last called her Meg . . .

'You don't have to come to the wedding, you know that . . . I haven't said much about it because it seems hardly fair — I wouldn't be hurt if you stayed at home — after all it is one time you would be fully justified in not being with me — Teresa isn't yours — she's another man's daughter . . . '

She talked slowly as if she wanted to drive home this fact, perhaps to prove his love even, to ensure his forgiveness . . .

The look in his eyes as he gave her his answer was proof enough that they had never been so close . . .

'My darling Margaret, to begin with, she is yours, therefore that makes her mine in a sense too, as if we are one, as the marriage service tells us, and it will be one of the proudest days of my life to stand beside you and to know at last you have come to terms with yourself, reached some kind of tranquillity . . . to me your happiness is all that really counts . . . ' he paused, 'I only wish I could have given away the bride, but I know you feel Sam should at least be allowed to do this, and I quite see your point . . . '

* * *

And so at last the great day came . . . the ancient little church was filled to bursting point, some chairs had even had to be brought from the village hall to supplement the pews and accommodate the overflowing congregation, for the Rossiter family were not only known and respected all over the county, but they had literally hundreds of relations, all of whom had had to be invited in case they should take offence at being left out . . . lifelong family feuds had started with less cause, Andy had said when Teresa had protested at the enormous crowd expected . . .

She had been overwhelmed too when she saw the presents that kept arriving — and any tiny pang of regret she might have had that she had no one she could call her own to send presents to the bride, was offset by Margaret's generosity and by the beautiful spode dinner service and Waterford glasses Sam had given her . . .

Andy's father had given them a small cottage up the lane from the farm itself, and his mother had had it completely decorated and furnished as her present to them . . . taking Teresa with her to Exeter to choose carpets and materials . . . it was like a fairy tale come true and Teresa kept thinking she would wake and find it had all been a perfect dream . . .

Margaret and Hugh arrived the day before the wedding, Linda and Tim were driving down the next morning . . . Teresa was almost beside herself with happiness and excitement, and after the first few moments, had got over her initial shyness with Hugh, who had seemed so stern and forbidding that first time she had met him . . .

But all that was forgotten in the past now, and Margaret was overjoyed to see the new air of confidence and serenity that seemed to shine out of her . . .

'You know,' she confided to Margaret as the latter helped her dress for the wedding, 'I was only thinking the other day, all this seemed to start happening from the moment you came into the hotel — little did I realise that first morning I brought your tea that anything like this could possibly happen to me — certainly nothing so marvellous as Andy . . . ' she hesitated for a moment, her face quite transformed, her cheeks flushed and her eyes shining . . .

Margaret thought, 'You're beautiful — quite beautiful — my own darling girl . . . ' the huge lump in her throat threatened to suffocate her as she looked at her . . .

Almost as if she'd read her thoughts

Teresa said, 'You helped me to make the most of my looks too, I was just an awful plain Jane — but I didn't care somehow — I think if no one else cares, then you don't care yourself . . . '

'Nonsense,' Margaret smiled, 'it's just that you hadn't learnt to make the best of yourself, and people are inclined to take one at one's own valuation in this busy world, they don't have much time to get under the skin . . . ' She bent down and arranged the soft folds of the white velvet so Teresa shouldn't read the naked feelings she knew must show in her eyes . . .

Slowly she got to her feet. 'There, all ready now, and quite the most beautiful bride I've ever seen . . . ' she kissed her lightly on the lips, 'I can only wish you all the happiness and joy there is in life,' she said softly, and added under her breath, please God let my daughter be happy as she deserves . . .

As the wedding march filled the church, Sam proudly walked with Teresa on his arm. He'd told Margaret not to worry, he'd be there always near at hand, to keep an eye on the girl . . . 'I'll miss her in the hotel, she was a good lass, with your training. I'd grown fond of her over the last few months,' he sighed, 'it was a double blow for poor old Sam, losing you both . . . '

Looking at his honest Yorkshire face with the stiff brush of greying hair like a badger's coat, and the eyes which were kind behind the shrewdness, she felt a moment of regret — poor old Sam, he was the one who had come out worse than anyone — and heaven knew he didn't deserve to . . .

'It's partly because she's your daughter Maggie, I can't ever forget that,' he sighed, 'you've been the catalyst my dear . . . ' he'd said when they were alone for a few moments the night before the wedding, 'you've changed me and that lass, both of us for the better I hope, shown us a way of life we didn't know existed . . . '

She looked round the rather shabby

office, thinking how much had happened in there in the few short weeks she'd used it — the upset over the money with Teresa — the phone call about Tim's accident, Sam telling her he loved her and wanted to marry her — and then Hugh's arrival and the bitter facts she had to reveal at last . . .

Now she touched his hand lightly and shook her head. 'No, I haven't been a catalyst in the true sense of the word, Sam, for that would mean I had changed others but remained the same myself — I've changed too in this case, almost beyond recognition . . . '

Now, as Teresa reached Andy's side and he turned with a look full of love and pride on his face, Hugh took Margaret's hand in his, and his eyes told her all she needed to know . . . that this was her great day — and yet she couldn't come out in her true colours as mother of the bride — she had had to play her part behind the scenes in seeing that all the arrangements ran smoothly . . . she's got to pretend just to be a friend at the church — he thought, the one who planned the reception, helped to make the dress — a matriarchal figure in all but actual name . . .

Margaret smiled up at him, her eyes filled with tears — but they were tears of pride and happiness as well as sadness — and on her other side — Linda and Tim, not quite sure what it was all about — but Tim had said admiringly after he'd been introduced to Teresa . . .

'You're a dark horse, Mum, keeping your young friend Teresa under your hat — she's a smashing bird . . . wish I'd met her before Andy — funny thing is, there's something vaguely familiar about her . . . '

Margaret smiled to herself, she hoped when he looked in the mirror he wouldn't realise what it was that was familiar, for surprisingly enough Teresa was very like him, both in colouring and the shape of her forehead and eyes . . .

She had had some moments of apprehension when she suggested he and Linda come to the wedding of 'the daughter of an old friend' as she put it — but they had both leapt at the chance — Tim because he was always ready for a party, and Linda because it meant a new outfit, and woman like, she adored weddings anyway . . . the three young people had got on well at once and Teresa had even told them to call and see her when she was installed at Rose Cottage after the honeymoon . . .

How strange it all was, Margaret thought . . . but now they were back at the Pack Horse, speeches were made, the cake cut and the champagne flowed freely — Hugh had made sure there was plenty of that as his contribution to the festivities . . .

At last Teresa had been up to change with Margaret's help, and the car was waiting to take them to the airport and away to Corfu . . .

As they drove away, all the goodbyes

said, the tears shed, Margaret stood for a moment on the steps of the Pack Horse, remembering so clearly the first time she'd walked up them, opened the door, and seen Sam — such a short while ago — and yet so much had happened.

And now her elder daughter had driven away from her — but they would still be friends — and Sam — she must say goodbye to him . . . goodbye to what might have been the perfect love that someday we all hope to find . . . or would it have been — was it just circumstances that made it seem so . . .

She turned quickly and went into the hotel where Hugh stood waiting for her — and Teresa's words echoed again in her mind . . .

'I've never known my mother — but I hope she was something like you . . . '

We do hope that you have enjoyed reading this large print book.

Did you know that all of our titles are available for purchase?

We publish a wide range of high quality large print books including:
Romances, Mysteries, Classics
General Fiction
Non Fiction and Westerns

Special interest titles available in large print are:
The Little Oxford Dictionary
Music Book, Song Book
Hymn Book, Service Book

Also available from us courtesy of Oxford University Press:
Young Readers' Dictionary
(large print edition)
Young Readers' Thesaurus
(large print edition)

For further information or a free brochure, please contact us at:
Ulverscroft Large Print Books Ltd.,
The Green, Bradgate Road, Anstey,
Leicester, LE7 7FU, England.
Tel: (00 44) **0116 236 4325**
Fax: (00 44) **0116 234 0205**

VISIONS OF THE HEART

Christine Briscomb

When property developer Connor Grant contracted Natalie Jensen to landscape the grounds of his large country house near Ashley in South Australia, she was ecstatic. But then she discovered he was acquiring — and ripping apart — great swathes of the town. Her own mother's house and the hall where the drama group met were two of his targets. Natalie was desperate to stop Connor's plans — but she also had to fight the powerful attraction flowing between them.

THE PERFECT GENTLEMAN

Liz Pedersen

When Laura agrees to help Anthony Christopher to deceive his family she has no idea how far the web of intrigue will extend, or how it will alter her life. His family is as unpleasant as he promised, but Laura drives away from his funeral thinking she has escaped their malicious clutches. However, this is not so. James Christopher is determined to discover what was behind his cousin's precipitate marriage. He despises Laura and hates the fact that he is attracted to her.

YESTERDAY'S LOVE

Stella Ross

Jessica's return from Africa to claim her inheritance of 'Simon's Cottage', and take up medicine in her home town, is the signal for her past to catch up with her. She had thought the short affair she'd had with her cousin Kirk twelve years ago a long-forgotten incident. But Kirk's unexpected return to England, on a last-hope mission to save his dying son, sparks off nostalgia. It leads Jessica to rethink her life and where it is leading.

THE DOCTOR WAS A DOLL

Claire Vernon

Jackie runs a riding-school and, living happily with her father, feels no desire to get married. When Dr. Simon Hanson comes to the town, Jackie's friends try to matchmake, but he, like Jackie, wishes to remain single and they become good friends. When Jackie's father decides to remarry, she feels she is left all alone, not knowing the happiness that is waiting around the corner.